# KING KILLA 2

Lock Down Publications and Ca$h
Presents

# King Killa 2

*A Novel by Vincent "Vitto" Holloway*

**Lock Down Publications**
P.O. Box 944
Stockbridge, Ga 30281 www.lockdownpublications.com

First Edition July 2023
Printed in the United States of America

*This is a work of fiction. Names, characters, places, and incidents
either are products of the author's imagination or are used
fictitiously. Any similarity to actual events or locales or persons,
living or dead, is entirely coincidental.*

**Lock Down Publications Like our page on Facebook: Lock
Down Publications @**
www.facebook.com/lockdownpublications.ldp

Book interior design by: **Shawn Walker**
Edited by: **Kiera Northington**

# Stay Connected with Us!

Text **LOCKDOWN** to 22828 to stay up-to-date with new releases, sneak peaks, contests and more... Thank you!

# Submission Guideline.

Submit the first three chapters of your completed manuscript to ldpsubmissions@gmail.com, subject line: Your book's title. The manuscript must be in a .doc file and sent as an attachment. Document should be in Times New Roman, double spaced and in size 12 font. Also, provide your synopsis and full contact information. If sending multiple submissions, they must each be in a separate email.

Have a story but no way to send it electronically? You can still submit to LDP/Ca$h Presents. Send in the first three chapters, written or typed, of your completed manuscript to:

LDP: Submissions Dept P.O.
Box 944
Stockbridge, Ga 30281

*DO NOT send original manuscript. Must be a duplicate.*

Provide your synopsis and a cover letter containing your full contact information.

Thanks for considering LDP and Ca$h Presents.

King Killa 2

## CHAPTER 1

"Daddy, Daddy…" Shinah kept repeating through her tears. She couldn't believe what she was seeing. She was holding onto him as if he would disappear if she let go, so she was squeezing him with all of her strength. "How are you alive? I saw Sincere with your watch. I knee…" She was rambling incoherently until her father held her hand, quieting her down as he smiled down at his only child.

"I'm real, baby girl," he told her with fatherly affection. He had missed her dearly, and not being there for her when she needed him the most was his biggest regret. "And I'm not going anywhere." He hugged her to his chest again, relishing in the feeling of her. "I'm so, so sorry Shinah," he whispered in her ear as he gassed over her shoulder at her mother, his ex-wife, with a look of pure loathing on his face that was almost palpable. The tension was felt by everyone in the room, even if they didn't understand what was going on.

"Aww, isn't this sweet," Charlene gritted through her pain as she sneered at him. As she tried to stop her wound from bleeding, she promised herself she would kill Shinah personally, this time for her disrespect.

"Charlene, you are an evil bitch, and I can't wait to give you exactly what you deserve," Bobby said in a voice so cold she actually shivered.

"It's amazing to me how you and your band of pawns think that you've beaten me." Charlene glanced around at everyone staring at her like she had two heads and chuckled. "I'm well positioned on my side of the board regardless of the predicament I'm in now," she added cryptically.

Sincere wanted to focus on what Charlene was saying, but all of this attention was solely on Shinah. Even after twenty plus years, she still took his breath away. "You're becoming a real expert at vanishing and reappearing in my life, Shinah," he said seriously as he took her in with his eyes.

Shinah was staring at him, confused about what to do now because she had no idea what would happen next. For half of her life she had thought of nothing else, trained for nothing else, than the sole purpose of killing him and her mother to avenge her father, but her father was alive and all of her plans were now obsolete.

"Vanishing!" she repeated, incredulous that he had the nerve to say that to her. "You're the one who vanished for over a week as my due date was imminent to 'handle business'," she said sarcastically as she made air quotes with here fingers. "Business that included a deal with my mother to murder my father, and in the process, you left me in the care of your flunky, who was also conspiring with my mother to murder me and your sons!" she screamed at him. She was upset, but more at herself because after so long he could still get under her skin.

Sincere smirked at her because he knew it too, which infuriated her all the more.

"Czar, I thought that your mother was locked up?" Dior asked curiously. She was so fascinated by what was unfolding around her. It was like a real life soap opera.

"She is locked up," he replied hesitantly. He was upset that he had been lied to his whole life.

"If you're our mother..." King was not overreacting to the situation as much as some, but a lot of things were not making any sense and he needed to put the puzzle together. "Where have you been our whole lives and why did you give us up for adoption?" he asked seriously.

Majestic was beyond livid. His whole life was a lie, and that was something he couldn't forgive his family for. "Did you know me were adopted?" he asked his sisters.

"Brudda, we dinna know," Star told him sadly.

Sky kept silent because she didn't know what to say. Truthfully, she was still in shock over the events unfolding in front of her eyes.

Majestic felt betrayed by everyone and everything he believed in and in a fit of rage, he snatched his father's necklace from around his neck and tossed it at his sister's feet. Star and Sky both gasped because they knew what that necklace meant to him. Sadly, Sky picked it up and pocketed it.

Shinah felt her heart breaking as the pain emanating from her sons pierced her soul. She knew that she had to explain herself but finding her father alive had disoriented her and she needed time to get herself together.

Sincere saw her indecision and decided to help her like he'd been doing since the day he met her. "Obviously, this story is for family only. So if you're not family, step into the V.I.P. room connected to this one and don't attempt to leave until told otherwise," he said in a quiet, authoritative tone that left no question whether he was asking or demanding.

No one in the room made a move to leave. Sincere saw this and grew incensed. He wasn't used to his orders being disregarded, but he understood that this was a unique situation and gave everyone who didn't know any better a pass for their ignorance. "In case you didn't hear me the first time, let me reiterate. If you're not of my bloodline, step into the next room and don't leave unless told otherwise by me. Don't confuse the situation," he added seriously. "I'm not the button. I'm the button pusher." He sat back down and waited to see if someone would really test his gangsta.

Dior wanted to stay with Czar for support, but also to be nosy. She looked over at him to see if she could read what he wanted her to do, but he was locked in on his parents. So she wasted no time following behind Bianca, who did not hesitate to leave the room.

"Son, are you straight?" Tango quietly asked King. He knew that the people in the room were on a different playing field, but his loyalty was abso lute, and if King said stay, then that's what he would do, despite who said otherwise.

"Yah, I'm a good, family," King replied with a smile, letting him know that he appreciated the show of loyalty. "I'll get with you in a few," he added reassuringly.

Tango nodded before filing out of the room. Star and Sky both looked to their brother for confirmation on what to do, but he refused to acknowledge them, and that hurt them badly, like he intended. Sky started crying as she followed her sister out of the room. Majestic felt his chest tighten at the sound of his sister crying, but he hardened his heart and let them go.

Pharaoh knew that Lion and the rest of his security team wouldn't leave him unattended unless he ordered them to do so. He gave the nod and watched as they filed out of the room.

"Mike Billy, that means you too," Sincere said seriously. The fact that he and Shinah had a past really bothered him, and he couldn't wait to find out what role he played in her life. "And don't get lost, because like the lady said, y'all have a lot to discuss," he added with a look that let him know that he was very interested in that discussion.

Mike Billy caught the look and knew that if Shinah revealed all that he did to her, then he was a dead man. Lucky for him that he always kept an exit strategy.

After the room was finally empty of every one who didn't matter, Sincere looked at Shinah and saw the appreciation in her eyes, but he wouldn't allow his feelings for her to block his common sense. Not this time. "Why did you choose to show up, Shinah?" he asked quietly.

She took a deep breath and turned to face her sons. "Majestic, Czar, King, and Pharaoh, I want you to know that I didn't leave you on purpose." She paused to take a deep breath because she was getting emotional. "I felt like——"

"This bitch is lying!" Charlene screamed out just to break up the Hallmark moment. Her plans were unraveling right before her eyes, but she wouldn't go down without a fight. She was still a Queen, albeit one without a king, but a queen nonetheless. "She was on drugs and doing all types——"

She was stopped short when Shinah spun around abruptly and punched her in the face, drawing blood. "Shut your mouth, Charlene," Shinah growled in her face. "Or I'll lay you right beside that piece of shit you were fucking," she added calmly. but deadly serious.

Charlene held her bloody lips and kept her mouth closed. The look in her daughter's eyes let her know that she would make good on her threat. She smiled, showing bloodstained teeth, because she liked the woman her daughter had become. But she still had to die.

Shinah shuddered a little when she saw that smile, but she put it out of her mind because she had more important things to get through to her chil dren. She turned and faced her boys once again before resuming her story. "At the time I met your father, I was starting to smoke laced blunts. I was tricked into smoking them by an ex, but I liked how they made me feel."

Sincere sighed because he still had regrets about not being able to help her, but he couldn't change the past, so he took a deep breath and tuned back into her story.

10

"Your father tried everything one could possibly try to help me." She gave him a small smile before continuing. "But I wasn't ready, and I betrayed his trust." She closed her eyes as her memoirs bombarded her. All the heat she had been harboring for Sincere the last couple of decades was replaced by the love she had stuffed deep down in the furthest recesses of her heart, and it was almost overwhelming to her senses. But she wanted – no, she needed - to tell her story so her boys could understand why she made the decisions that altered all of their lives. "I ran away from him and his help because I was in love with the way crack made me feel. I stole his drugs and money before I ran. The next time he saw me, I was pregnant with you. When I found out I was pregnant, I quit cold turkey. I was determined to bring a healthy baby into this world."

"So you didn't know that you were pregnant with quadruplets?" King asked curiously. He found himself being drawn in despite his reservations about the situation.

Shinah graced him with a sad smile before continuing. "No, I didn't know until I was pushing you out. I didn't want to know anything about the baby - or babies, in this case - because I just wanted a healthy surprise. As I was waiting to give birth to you, Sincere was by my side every second until he had to go out of town, as I alluded to earlier."

Sincere closed his eyes in regret as he remembered having to leave her.

"He left me under the care of that man." She pointed to the dead body of Jay Jay, still lying where he was shot. "One day as I was preparing to go see you boys in the nursery, I heard Jay Jay plotting with someone to kill me. Of course I was terrified and panicking, but despite my fear, I managed to shuffle my way to the door to see who he was talking to. Who I saw confused and shocked me." Shinah closed her eyes as she relived that day in her mind. "It was my mother, casually having a conversation with a person she shouldn't even know about killing her only child, her only daughter. I made a noise that I thought would get me caught, so I painfully made my way back to my bed just in time to fake sleep. As I lay there, my mother was imploring Jay Jay to slip into my room and smother me with my pillow. The only thing that saved me was the nurse coming to check on me. I had also heard her tell Jay Jay that my father was dead."

Bobby placed his hand on his daughter's shoulder to give her what little comfort he could, He couldn't imagine all of the things she had to endure when he wasn't there to protect her, his biggest regret in life. Hearing her recount how her mother had plotted to kill them both had his blood boiling, but he kept his peace because Charlene would get what was coming to her.

Shinah grabbed her father's hand and held it in her own as she continued her story. "I was still so weak from giving birth, but I knew that I had to get out of there or I would die in the same hospital I had just given birth in. So I asked the nurse if I could go down to the nursery for you boys. At first she was adamant about going with me, but I needed to be alone for my plan to work. So I convinced her that I needed some alone time with my children as a mother, and she agreed. After reassuring her that I was strong enough, I rolled down in the wheelchair they provided and just stared at my four miracles." "You just left us there," Czar stated angrily. He was picturing the life he could've had compared to the way he grew up, and it pissed him off.

"I had no choice," Shinah replied to his deadly anger. "I was still weak from massive blood loss during birth and at the same time trying not to get murdered. You and your brothers were still hooked up to all of these wires and machines. You looked so fragile and small that I thought if I took you with me, you would surely die. I had no way of taking care of you. Hell, I didn't have a way to take care of myself. I really thought that you would have a better chance at life without me because I felt useless as a woman and I didn't think I had what it took to be a good mother. I wanted to murder my own mother for having my father killed." She cast an evil glare at Charlene before continuing. "I left the hospital and managed to steal a car. I was parked across from my parents' home, ready to avenge my father or die trying, when I saw Sincere pull up bearing a gift for Charlene, my father's watch that he always wore whenever he went out of town." Sincere remembered that moment vividly and could only imagine the grief she caused her. He wished that he could've told her what was going on, but he wasn't afforded the opportunity to do so because she was gone when he returned. So much of his life - their lives - would've been different if only he hadn't sold his soul for a dollar.

"I thought that my father was dead and that the father of my newborns was the one who murdered him. I didn't know what to do, but I knew that I had to go underground to recuperate and put a plan together. I went back to the hospital to get you when it quieted down, but you were already gone. It took me years before I was able to find out that Charlene took you from the hospital and even longer to track down the orphanage you were adopted from, but by that time, you were fully embedded in your new lives, and the life I was living wasn't fit for a child. "After I saw that you all were safe, revenge was the only thing on my mind. Over the years, I've done things to make your lives easier where I could, but I chose to stay in the shadows for my safety as well as yours. When I realized that other hands were pulling strings in your lives, I had to speed up my timetable, and here we are. I'm not coming into this expecting much, but I would like the chance to know my sons. Our family history is dark and twisted, but I love you more than life itself and I'm proud of the men you've become." As much as she tried not to cry, she couldn't stop the tears from cascading down her cheeks.

\*\*\*

"What are they saying?" Dior asked Bianca for what seemed like the hundredth time. Nervously, she paced the room as she thought about the events that had unfolded so fast. She couldn't believe that there were three more Czars on the earth. She could barely deal with the one, so she definitely wouldn't know what to do with four.

"Bitch, if you don't be quiet so I can hear what's being said," Bianca snapped in irritation as she put her ear back to the door. She was frustrated because despite her best efforts to eavesdrop, she couldn't hear a thing.

"You know that these rooms are soundproof, right?" Tango put that in the air with a smirk on his face.

Bianca blushed before rolling her eyes at him.

Dior mugged him and also rolled her eyes at him, but they both had the decency to look embarrassed.

Tango couldn't blame them for trying to find out what was going on because he wanted to know himself, but he trusted King to put him on point when the time came. In the meantime, he kept his eyes on the people in the room with him. The two Jamaican sisters, Star and Sky, were consoling each other and not worried about anything else. He turned and locked eyes with the man called Lion. After doing a bid up north, he could recognize a killer, and this man was certified. Tango considered himself a thoroughbred, but he wouldn't want to get into it with him. As much as he hated himself for it, he broke eye contact first. Lion gave him a feeling he didn't like: fear.

\*\*\*

"So let me get this straight," Czar started in a state of bewilderment "Our father sold you crack - our mother; you both fell in love; you betrayed him, you took off, and the next time he saw you, you were pregnant, presumably with us." He waved his arm at his brothers. "While in the hospital waiting to give birth, our grandmother was plotting with our father to kill our grandfather, who's really not dead, while at the same time plotting to kill you with our father's right hand man. Somehow, we all ended up in Miami, at this club, at the same time. You, our father, our grandparents, and my brothers, basically our entire bloodline. If I wasn't standing here witnessing this, I would have to be an idiot to think that this is a coincidence."

"Somebody has to have some really big hands to pull all of these strings at the same time," King stated seriously as he caught onto Czar's line of reasoning.

"Damn, my grand babies are smarter than they look," Charlene said sarcastically before she started laughing uncontrollably at everyone's puzzled expressions. She noticed no one really paying attention to her, and that's exactly how she wanted it. She knew that if she could get to Jay unnoticed then she would show everyone a time Queen.

Sincere had been trying to put all of the pieces to this puzzle together from the very beginning, but the one thing that kept eluding him was how they all ended up at the club, at that moment. That was, until his son started laying it all out, then it hit him like lightning. He looked over at Charlene and noticed her fumbling with something, but it didn't register because if he was right, then they were all in danger. He locked eyes with Bobby and knew that they were on the same page. He stood up abruptly, causing everyone in the room to look at him in either confusion or suspicion.

"I need everyone to listen to me," he announced seriously. "We have to get out of this building right now."

Shinah was about to question him when movement in her peripheral caught her attention. She looked in the direction and to her complete shock, saw Charlene with a gun in her hand, pointed directly at her. Somehow during the commotion, her mother had managed to retrieve the gun Jay Jay had on his person when he was murdered and there was nothing she could do.

***

Charlene knew that she was the best Queen on the board and as soon as she eliminated her troublesome daughter, there would be no one left to dispute that claim. She realized that as her finger tightened on the trigger, she didn't feel the expected elation she usually felt when she removed an enemy from the playing field. She actually felt sadness, which shocked her, but didn't stop her finger from pulling the trigger.

***

Shinah felt as if she was stuck in quicksand as she watched her mother pulling the trigger. After all of these years and all of her plans for revenge, her mother would still win, and there was nothing she could do about it.

Bobby noticed that his daughter wasn't focused on the room, but on her mother. When he looked over and saw the gun in Charlene's hands, he reacted without hesitation, diving in front of Shinah just as a gun went off.

"Daddy, noooo!" Shinah screamed as she searched his body for a gunshot wound. She didn't know what she would do if he died trying to save her life after just getting him back.

"Baby girl, I'm okay. I'm not shot," Bobby said slowly as he sat up.

Confused, Shinah looked up at her mother and noticed the gaping wound in her chest. She looked back and saw her son Majestic with a gun still pointed her way.

"Ye should have killed de snake as soon as you laid eyes pon she," he responded to the question in her eyes. "Blood makes ye related. Loyalty makes ye family," he added seriously.

King, Czar, and Pharaoh did not speak it aloud because they all were thinking the same thing. Shinah couldn't exactly argue with that logic, but she hated that her son had to be the one to kill his grandmother, even if he was saving her life. She looked down at her mother and saw that she was struggling to say something with her dying breath. She kneeled down and put her ear as close to her mother's lips as she could to hear what she had to say.

"My…child…will…avenge…me," Charlene gurgled before the light left her eyes.

I'm her only child, Shinah thought, con-

fused. She looked over at her father with a puzzled expression on her face.

"What did she say, baby?" Bobby asked her gingerly. He was careful with her feelings because despite the horrific things Charlene had done to her, she was still her mother at the end of the day.

Shinah was about to repeat what she heard Charlene say with her dying breath, but decided against it. "Nothing at all, Daddy," she said quietly. Just some crazy ramblings of a remorseful dying old woman, she thought to herself sadly.

"As I said before, we need to  leave now," Sincere repeated quietly in the midst of the tragic events that had unfolded minutes, before but if he was right about who might be pulling strings, then the danger was real and they had to act fast. "Everyone in this room needs to show up tomorrow night around eight at the Four Seasons hotel penthouse suite downtown. We have a lot to discuss." He said this last part while looking directly at Shinah. She didn't avert her eyes because she knew that she had a lot to answer for, but so did he. "Handle your affairs with your loved ones, and one last thing." He took a deep breath and exhaled slowly.

"Don't die."

## CHAPTER 2

Mike Billy was biting his nails down to the quick as he sat in his private office, watching the meeting Sincere was having with Shinah. He was going crazy wondering what was being said and mentally lambasting himself for not also installing audio equipment in each of the VIP rooms like he started to do when he had the cameras put in. He needed to know what Shinah intended to do about their past history and if she planned on telling Sincere. He knew firsthand how ruthless Sincere was and what would happen to him if he ever learned about the things he did to Shinah when he was running his parents' small motel decades ago. He vividly remembered every illicit detail of what he did to Shinah against her will. Hell, he even dreamed about it.

Sitting there in the privacy of his office, he felt himself getting an erection as he watched her on the video monitor, but it instantly deflated as he watched one of her sons kill Charlene. The implications of her death on his premises had him panicking. He was riveted to the screen to see what else would unfold. He breathed a sigh of relief when he noticed everyone leaving, but grimaced when he realized that there were two dead bodies left behind for him to dispose of. He waited another ten minutes to see if anyone would double back before calling a discreet cleaning service to remove the bodies from his properly.

He left his office and walked into the elevator that would take him back to the V.I.P. room. Before the doors closed, a hand shot through, causing them to open back up. Mike Billy looked up and felt this bladder loosen when he saw who was stepping onto the elevator with him.

"H-hi, Miss S-Salvatore," he stuttered out of fear. He wasn't surprised that she didn't respond to him because she never did. In fact, he couldn't remember ever hearing her speak at all. He couldn't figure her out, and that put him at a disadvantage - a place he wasn't used to operating from when it came to women. She was unbelievably gorgeous, but she had a menacing air about her that quite frankly frightened him. Sometimes he found himself staring at her because she kind of reminded him of Shinah, and until tonight, he thought he would never see Shinah again. So he fantasized as he watched Miss Salvatore, but he stopped after she caught him. It was like she knew what he was thinking, and the look she gave him made him not want to get caught staring at her again. It never crossed his mind what she was doing at the club until it was too late.

Before he could stop them, the doors to the elevator opened. He was watching her face and when she saw the carnage the look of rage that crossed her visage caused his bladder to loosen. He was so terrified that he didn't even see her pull out a gun.

"What happened?" she asked quietly as she fought to control her emotions.

Mike Billy temporarily forgot his fear when he heard her voice. It shocked him in its softness, but it never lost its edge. The songlike lilt of her voice could confuse you into thinking that she was delicate, but anyone who knew her knew better. He also detected a slight accent, but he couldn't place it. He looked up and shook himself out of his reverie when he saw the fire in her eyes.

"I can show you better than I can tell you," he said as his fear returned to full force.

Miss Salvatore just nodded her assent as she gripped her gun tightly.

Mike Billy hurriedly pressed the button to send the elevator back to his private office. When he noticed her staring at him, he followed her gaze and reddened in embarrassment when he saw that she had noticed his unfortunate accident when he couldn't control his bladder when the doors opened up. He made his way to his office to get away from her disapproving gaze and to show her that he had nothing to do with what happened in that V.I.P. room. He was rewinding the video to play when she walked into the office and closed the door behind her. He pressed play and hoped that she realized that he wasn't culpable for what she was about to witness. For the next fifteen minutes, she watched the video over and over again, rewinding and fast forwarding at her leisure, turning him into a nervous wreck as he awaited her verdict.

"Who else has seen this?" Miss Salvatore asked calmly. Looking at her, one couldn't see the rage boiling right beneath the surface.

Mike Billy breathed a sigh of relief when he heard the tone of her voice. It didn't sound as if she was upset with him, so he relaxed as much as he could. She still frightened him. "Only you and me," he answered, trying to be as helpful as possible.

"How many copies have you made?" she asked as she locked eyes with him.

Mike Billy swallowed his nervousness and quickly broke eye contact with her. "This is the only copy," he said quietly. If he had been more observant, he would've known that he was about to die. Without hesitation, Miss Salvatore raised her gun and silenced Mike Billy forever. She wasted no time removing the CD with the video on it and making sure no other copies were made. After disabling the cameras in the V.I.P. rooms, she made her way back to the elevator. She pressed the button to return to the V.I.P. room and thought about what she had seen on the video. Her thoughts would've surprised all who knew her because she was known to be calculating and ruthless, but she was actually excited by what she had seen on the video. She couldn't wait to make the proper introductions.

The doors opened up, and her eyes instantly picked the body of the woman who deserved her scorn, but also her admiration. Their relationship was complicated, but she didn't like how she was left behind like trash. As she stepped out of the elevator, she gripped her gun tighter as her eyes swept over the room, taking in every detail. When she arrived at the bodies, she never spared a glance at the man lying beside Charlene. In her mind, he was inconsequential. She knelt and let her eyes drink in this once proud woman as if she wanted to remember every detail.

Even though there wasn't anyone in the room with her besides the two dead bodies, she still felt the need to whisper, "You summoned me too late, but I promise you, Mother, that your death won't be in vain."

She stood up and pulled out a cell phone. She hit a button and waited for an answer. "Burn it down," she said and then hung up. She dropped the phone to the floor and stomped on it.

Before leaving she glanced at her mother one last time. She exited the same way she remembered everyone on the video did. She had a family reunion to attend.

## CHAPTER 3

The car was silent as Bianca, Dior and Czar left the club and made their way back to the room. Bianca, who was driving, kept looking in the rearview at Czar. He was sitting in the backseat, lost in his own thoughts. She looked over at her best friend Dior in the passenger seat, fidgeting and biting her lip. She wanted to laugh because she could tell that Dior was battling between being nosy and respecting Czar's privacy. She knew her friend like the back of her hand so she wasn't surprised when Dior turned around in her seat and started questioning him.

"Baby, are you okay?" she asked in concern. Bianca caught Czar's eyes in the rearview mirror and they both laughed.

"What?" Dior asked in aggravation. She knew that they were laughing at her, but for what, she didn't know.

"Bitch, stop fronting and just ask the questions you've been dying to ask since we left the club," Bianca said, humor lacing every word. "Whatever, bitch," Dior replied with a frown. "So baby, how do you feel about there being three more you in the world?" she asked curiously. Czar looked bewildered for a few seconds before replying, "There's only one me." He didn't blink for what seemed like a minute to let her know that he was serious.

Dior rolled her eyes at his arrogant answer, but it was one of the things she loved about him. "Seriously though, to go from thinking that you're an only child to having three identical brothers has to be strange," she said, as she wondered what four of her would be like. We would definitely run the world, she thought wrongly. "Do you think y'all will get along?" she asked as she studied him. "We'll see," Czar said nonchalantly in his New Orleans drawl.

Dior sucked her teeth and rolled her eyes at him before turning around in her seat in frustration. No matter how nonchalant Czar was acting, he was wondering the same thing. Did his brothers think like him? How did they move? Did they have the same habits? Same interest? The questions were endless, but he was excited to find out the answers.

\*\*\*

"Son, that shit was bananas!" Tango ex- claimed as he looked over at King. He was sitting in the passenger seat as they sped through the streets of Miami. "You have three niggas in this world who look exactly like you," he added in disbelief.

King didn't respond as he navigated traffic. He was watching his rearview mirror to make sure they weren't being followed. The meeting he had just left at the club with his surprise family had him feeling like a pawn in someone's game, so he was watching to make sure they didn't get caught slipping. Even though he never acknowledged Tango's statement, he was in just as much disbelief as his partner. First, he found out that he was adopted. Second, he found out that he had three identical brothers. Third, he met his mother and father. And last but definitely not least, some unknown enemy was trying to murder him. Whoever it was would soon find out that he wasn't named King for no reason.

Tango kept this mouth shut because he knew the King wouldn't answer him. They had been roommates for years up north and he knew that King was in his own world, plotting and planning. He just sat back and got his mind right for the fireworks he was sure to come.

\*\*\*

Majestic sat in the backseat of his sister's car, still broken about being adopted. He couldn't believe that his father - no, the man who raised him - had lied to him his whole life. Everything he knew came from that man, and to now find out it was all based on a lie was devastating. He felt his sisters peeping at him and he knew he was hurting them with his silence, but he wasn't ready for all of the questions he knew they would hit him with. When he was ready, he would let them know that regardless of the situation, they would always be his family - if not by blood, then by deed and loyalty. No matter how upset he was at being adopted and lied to about it, he would never turn his back on them. He was excited about having three brothers, but he would reserve his love and loyalty until he knew how they were built. Besides, blood only made you related. Loyalty made you family.

***

Pharaoh was ecstatic that he had three identical brothers. Twenty-four hours ago, he thought he didn't have any family left in this world, but now he had met his mother, father, grandparents, and brothers all in one night. He couldn't reconcile the fact that his birth father was the same man who inadvertently changed his life the day he sent hitmen to his graduation to murder his adoptive parents. Or did he? He recalled the line of reasoning his two brothers Czar and King put into everyone's mind about some unseen force behind the scene pulling the string like some master puppeteer. He couldn't discount their claims because since he was thrust into the role of kingpin, he had become aware of a world that he didn't know existed, let alone operated with immunity from the law and law abiding citizens alike. The old Pharaoh, the one whose innocence was still intact, would've been shocked at what he had seen tonight but the new Pharaoh, the one who was forced into a seat at the table made up of the grimiest and slimiest of the underworld, took everything in stride because he now knew the power he wielded, and anyone in the dark about that would soon be brought into the light.

***

Sincere, Shinah and her father Bobby were riding in the back of Sincere's chauffeured limo in complete silence, everyone lost in their own thoughts.

This isn't happening, Shinah thought desperately as she looked at her father sitting calmly in front of her, a man that she thought was dead by the hand of the man she could feel staring at her intently. She was afraid to look at Sincere because nothing was going as planned.

She thinks I'm going to make this easy on her, Sincere thought angrily. But she had another thing coming.

Bobby was alternating his gaze between his daughter and Sincere, wondering how this was going to play out. Sincere was of a dying breed and he respected him more than he could ever express. When he told him about the history between him and his daughter and what he tried to do there, that respect blossomed into love. Over the years, he had come to see him as the son he never had. But Shinah was his daughter, his princess, and he would side with her no matter the consequences of that decision. He knew his daughter like the back of his hand and he knew that the problem was deeper than they all knew. So he would sit back and let it all play out. "Stop the car," Shinah said suddenly. She had come up with a plan. She just had to hope that it worked. "What!" Sincere and Bobby both shouted at the same time. They were both looking at her like she had grown two heads.

"Stop the car," Shinah repeated again in a calmer tone. Now that she was initiating her place, she would see it through.

"I guess it's in your nature to run," Sincere said angrily to disguise his disappointment. He picked up the car phone and bid the driver to pull over.

Shinah heard the disappointment in his voice and wanted to address it, but that would come later. "Daddy, I need you to come with me," she pleaded as she opened the door to exit the limo. "Wait." Sincere was confused. Inside he was panicking because he wasn't in control, and that wasn't a position he was used to being in. "What's happening?"

"I know you have no reason to believe anything I'm getting ready to tell you, but it's the truth." Shinah looked him in his eyes, hoping to convey her sincerity. "I had planned to kill you tonight, but my father still being alive threw me in a tailspin. I'm grateful. You didn't murder him for whatever reason, but for two plus decades, I thought he was dead and that you and my mother killed him. It's a lot I need to say to you because the water is deeper beneath the surface. It's been twenty-five years, but I promise to tell you everything. To be honest, I'm behind the eight ball because nothing has gone as planned." "When it comes to you, plans never go right," Sincere said seriously.

Shinah smiled ruefully at his statement because she knew better than most that his plans for her never went according to plan. "I promise you that me and Daddy will be at the meeting. Now that I've gotten our sons back in my life, I will cherish every minute," she said resolutely.

"Our sons" echoed through Sincere's mind as he stared at the love of his life. Foolish or not, he couldn't seem to be able to deny her. So with a slight nod, he acquiesced to her need to set things right.

Shinah released the breath she didn't realize she was holding when she saw that he wasn't going to fight with her on this. Without another word, she got out of the limo and awaited her father.

"Everything will work out, son," Bobby told Sincere sympathetically before following his daughter. "It always does, old man," Sincere replied quietly as the limo pulled off.

"What's going on, Shinah?" Bobby asked his daughter as he watched the limo until he could no longer see the taillights. "All will be repealed soon, Daddy," Shinah said distractedly as she pulled out her cell phone and fired off a quick text message. She had heard the term of endearment her father used for Sincere and it had her even more anxious than she was before. She looked at her father, her Superman, and knew that he wouldn't be able to save her this time.

Bobby saw the look of despair on his daughter's face and pulled her in for a hug.

Shinah fell into his embrace and released the tears she had been holding in all night. "Daddy, everything I've done was based on the thought that you were dead," she sobbed into his chest.

"I know, baby, and everything will be okay," he said soothingly as he patted her back to calm her down. Shinah sighed and stepped out of his embrace, wiping her tears from her face. "I don't know if Sincere and our sons will be able to forgive me for this," he added sadly.

Before Bobby could ask her what she meant, a blacked-out Cadillac Escalade SUV pulled to a stop at the curb in front of them.

"This is us, Daddy," Shinah told him before opening the back door and sliding into the SUV.

Bobby didn't know what his daughters was into, but he had been in the game a long time and he knew that she was playing in the big leagues. The bulletproof SUV and the two African bodyguards could attest to that. He looked at his daughter, but she was texting on her phone and not paying him any attention. He took this time to really look at her and unseen to him before were the war wounds. She didn't have visible scars, but there was a hardness about her that was only recognizable to those who knew her best. It broke his heart because he didn't protect his daughter from the monsters under her bed like he had promised all those years ago when she was a little girl. He vowed that as long as he had breath in his body, he would protect her from the monsters in the dark, even if he himself was one said monster. He glanced out of the tinted window and noticed that they had entered an affluent neighborhood where every mini mansion was surrounded by gates and walls protecting the precious cargo inside. But the residence they pulled up to was different. These replicas of the men chauffeuring their SUV emerged from the darkness and surveyed the occupants of their vehicle. He noticed that his daughter was shown the utmost deference by the soldiers. He kept his peace and continued to observe because he had a feeling things were about to take a turn. After satisfying themselves that no imminent danger was present, words were whispered into wrist mics and the ornate, wrought iron gates swung open. The opulence of the grounds let him know that they were dealing with generational wealth. He glanced over at his daughter and noticed that she was fidgeting, letting him know that she was nervous about something. He wondered what it was, but once again, he kept his peace. When they pulled to a stop in front of the mansion, two more carbon copy soldiers rushed over to open their doors.

"Welcome home, Mrs. Bandele," one of the soldiers greeted her.

"Thank you, Malik," Shinah replied to the young, loyal soldier. He was one of her favorites. She glanced at her father and could tell that he had a lot of questions. All of them would be answered sooner rather than later.

"Your daughter has been asking for you nonstop," Malik informed her as he led them into the house. Shinah grimaced because she knew that her father had overheard that statement, but she didn't turn around to gauge his reaction. The closer she got to the house, the more nervous she became. Before she was able to enter the residence properly, she heard little feet running towards her. Despite her nervousness, she found herself smiling when she saw her daughter running full speed towards her.

"Mommy!" her daughter screamed joyfully before launching herself into her arms. "Did you miss me?" she asked hopefully.

Shinah laughed because no matter where she went and no matter how long she was gone, her daughter greeted her with the same enthusiasm and questions. "Of course Mommy missed you," she replied before kissing her cheek. She looked over her daughter's shoulder and saw her son and husband standing there, but they weren't focused on her. All of their attention was focused behind her. She looked back and saw that her father's face held a visage of rage that scared her. It was like he was a different person right then and he had a faraway look in his eyes as

if he was remembering something from a time long past. "Something on your mind, old man?" Moosa asked seriously. He didn't like the way he was looking and wouldn't hesitate to snuff his lights out despite walking in with his mother.

Shinah looked at her hot-headed son sharply, letting him know to watch his tongue.

Moosa grimaced, but he bit his tongue. He would never disrespect his mother.

Shinah looked back to her father and wondered what was wrong. She grabbed his hand and looked into his eyes to bring him back, but it was as if he was looking through her instead of at her.

"Wife."

"Yes, husband," she replied to the man who loved her beyond what she deserved. Moses Bandele was staring at her with a look she felt that was only reserved for him and she understood why. "Who is this man you have brought around our family?" he asked curiously. He was completely at ease because he knew that Shinah wouldn't put their family in any danger, but he knew the mission she was on, so he was cautious. Besides, a person would be foolish to bring trouble to his doorstep.

"Yeah, Mommy, who is this man?" Gifted, her daughter, asked parroting her father. She reached out and touched the face of the man in question before her mother could stop her.

Shinah looked at her father and saw that the touch of her daughter had put a spark back into his eyes.

She took this opportunity to introduce everyone and relieve the tension hanging over the room, "Husband, Moosa, and Gifted, I would like you to meet my father, Bobby Lloyd," she said calmly. All of her carefully laid plans were out the window. So now all she could do was go with the flow and do it with grace.

"I thought he was dead," Moosa said incredulously.

He looked to his mother for answers.

"I have two papas?" Gifted squealed delightedly.

Everyone laughed, lightening the mood somewhat. Bobby even smiled, but he couldn't get over how small the world really was. "You're Ahmad Bandele's boy, right?" he asked his daughter's husband. "I am," Moses replied calmly, wondering how this man knew his father. To outsiders, he looked perfectly at peace but to those who knew him, especially his wife Shinah, the look in his eyes was the calm before the storm.

King Killa 2

## CHAPTER 4

Terror was sitting in the living room of his palatial estate trying to drown his pain with a bottle of Jack Daniels. All of the drapes were drawn tight and the lights were off to create a dark and gloomy atmosphere that matched his mood. Ever since Chaka had murdered his family, he had been holed up in his compound, trying to figure out how he was going to kill Chaka before she killed him. He had no delusions about going toe to toes with her because he had seen her do some unbelievable things as his chief enforcer, and now she had declared war against him. So unless he found a way to put her down, his life was on a countdown, ticking towards his demise. He was about to take another swig of his Jack when he felt cold hard steel being pressed against the back of his head. He saw his life flash before his eyes and let his bladder loosen. "Please, please, Chaka, men don't want to die. Men will pay you whatever you want. Please don't kill men," he begged as tears slid down his face. Cha'nel looked down at the man on the oth- er end of her gun and shook her head in disgust. Her husband, her heartbeat, had died for this sniveling coward and she was tempted to put a bullet through his head and be done with it, but she needed information first and foremost. Then he would die. "Remember me?" she asked in heavily accented English.

Terror heard the voice and started crying even harder because his dirty deeds had finally come to the light. Now everything made sense. He had hired Rah'mel and Cha'nel to kill Chaka after she took care of the Livingstones because she knew too much and she was dangerous, so she had to go - or so he thought. The cleanup must've gone bad and Chaka figured that he was behind it. Hence the murders of his family. Chaka must've killed or maimed Cha'nel's husband and that's why she was there holding a pistol to his head. She had figured out that he had withheld pertinent information concerning their target and the mission went away. Now he would die for it.

"Shut up, pitiful boy," Cha'nel said harshly. The crying was grinding on her nerves and had her ready to kill him just to shut him up.

"Wat are ye doing 'ere?" Terror asked respectfully after he got his crying under control.

"You know exactly why I'm here," she growled. Just thinking about her love had her ready to kill any and everything who looked at her wrong. "You sent us in blind and it cost me my husband." She paused as she took a second with her emotions. "I saw him in the hospital and the injuries my love had were done by a professional – a professional you sent us after blind." Her fury caused her to hit him with the butt of her gun, knocking him out.

*** 

Pharaoh watched as his three brothers were ushered into the villa he was renting while in Miami and felt his pulse quicken. As he studied them, he noticed that they all had the same mannerisms. He wondered if they all liked and disliked the same things. We'll find out soon enough, he thought as he stood up to greet his brothers. "Glad you could make it," he said, surprised at the excitement he was feeling. He was genuinely happy to have brothers in his life. As he shook each one of their hands he was shocked when Czar pulled him in for a half hug. "We're brothers. So cut out all of the professional handshaking shit," he teased when he noticed the shock on his face after he released him from the embrace.

Pharaoh rubbed his hand over his head as he chuckled in embarrassment. When he heard them, his brothers laughing at him, he joined in and it felt good. He was glad he had called this meeting. "I do the same thing when I'm embarrassed about something," King told Pharaoh when the laughing subsided.

"Do what?" he asked, confused.

"Rub my hand over my head," King said with a smirk.

"Mem do dat also," Majestic continued in wonder. Despite his anger over being lied to about his adoption, he was elated to have three brothers.

They all looked to Czar, who nodded his head in agreement that he also did the same thing. For the next couple of hours, they charted their similarities into a bond that would prove unbreakable. Despite not growing up together, they were comfortable with each other. They were amazed that four men raised by different parents, in different places, were essentially the same person.

"This is crazy," Czar said in amazement. "I'm a force by myself, have taken over states with my guns or product, but with four of us on the same agenda, I don't see how we can be stopped," he added seriously.

"I feel the same way, bro," King said as he was thinking along the same lines.

Pharaoh looked at his brothers and knew that he had made the right decision. He was taught to always take care of family, and who could be more of his family than the three men sitting in the room with him? He reached down into the briefcase lying at his feet and pulled out three folders. He set them on the table and looked them in their eyes, because what he was about to reveal would change their lives forever. "I grew up with an affluent lifestyle." "You mean rich," Czar cracked with a smirk.

All of the brothers chuckled a little before Pharaoh continued.

"When I was growing up, I never worried about money because I was always given everything. I hated it because I didn't know if I could do anything for myself." His voice grew more grave with each word. "That is, until my adoptive parents were murdered." He took a deep breath to get his emotions under control.

No one said anything, but they all wore the same somber expressions.

"After their deaths, I inherited everything, including knowledge I wasn't equipped to handle, but it was imperative that I did so because not only was my life on the line, but my parents' legacy was in jeopardy also. The man I took care of back at the club was the man who executed my adoptive parents. Our birth father was supposed to be next because he gave the order, but then we found out he helped create us, so I spared him. I say all of that to say that before tonight, I didn't think I had any family left in this world but now. I have three identical brothers who I'm assuming had it harder than I did coming up. So I made the decision to put my brothers, my reflections, in positions to walk the earth' as giants amongst men." He slid the folders to them and sat back, awaiting their reactions.

"Is this fa real?" Czar asked in disbelief. His heart was racing because all of his dreams were now a reality.

"Of course," Pharaoh replied with a smile.

"Brudda, mem speechless," Majestic said seriously. He wasn't one for displaying his emotions, but what his brother had just bestowed upon him had him in his feelings.

King was shocked, but he kept it in check. He was just handed generational wealth from a brother he had just met. This gesture of loyalty earned him loyalty for a lifetime. "When did you have time to put all of this together?" he asked curiously. "Like you said before, you didn't know about us before tonight. So how did you do this after midnight on a Friday night?'

Pharaoh smiled at his brothers because they were happy. He could tell they didn't expect anything of this magnitude, but there was no way he would allow his brothers to go without. "Anything is possible brother with the right connections," he said cryptically. "Especially when you own a percentage of the bank," he added arrogantly.

"I heard that hot shit," King replied with a smirk. "So, what's next?" Czar asked as he contemplated his options. His life had changed drastically over the last twenty-four hours. He went from fighting for his life and catching bodies all through the south to being in a whole new tax bracket. This was a world that he wasn't familiar with, but he was a real nigga and he would always rise to the occasion. "Have any of you ever heard of the Council?" Pharaoh asked seriously.

None of them had.

"What is the Council?" King asked seriously. He could tell by the look on his brother's face that they were serious.

"What I'm about to tell you is only known to a select few individuals, and even being in possession of this information could get you murdered." He looked each one of his brothers in their eyes to convey the seriousness of what he was saying. "So, I will understand if any of you want to leave. No grudges held and no hard feelings for any who choose to leave. Once in, there is no out. It's life and death literally. So what's it going to be?" He was pretty sure of what their responses would be, but he needed to be sure.

King, Czar, and Majestic all knew that their lives were no longer singular events. Their destinies were now intertwined. None of them said a word, but no one got up to leave either,

Pharaoh looked at his brothers and felt a strong sense of gratitude because he knew that he was no longer alone. He smiled, because life was about to get real interesting. "Okay then, my brothers, let's get started."

\*\*\*

Terror was rudely awakened by ice cold water being thrown in his face. He was groggy, trying to remember what had happened, but he was struggling. He tried to move but to his surprise, he was tied to a chair in his kitchen. He was frantically trying to get himself untied because he thought that Chaka had come back to finish him off and he didn't want to go out like this. He stopped moving suddenly when he saw movement out of the corner of his eye. For some reason, that calmed him down because Chaka didn't play with her food. She would've killed him where he stood for his betrayal. Trying him up wasn't her style. He was still trying to figure out who did this to him when his captor stepped out of the shadows. When he saw Cha'nel, one half of the deadliest assassin duos in existence, he knew that this deceitfulness had finally come to the light.

"Wakey, wakey, snakey, snakey," Cha'nel said snidely.

Her reference about him being a snake confirmed her agenda.

"Why did you lie?" she asked seriously. She tried to keep her temper in check because she needed information and she wouldn't get it if she kept knocking him out.

"Wat do ye mean?" he asked nervously.

The only response he got to his question was the sound of her gun being cocked.

"Okay, okay." Terror knew that his life wasn't in his hands, so he decided to be upfront and honest and then he would pray for the best. "Mem dinna tink dat ye would take de contract if mem told ye how it was." He knew that his tactics were underhanded but he never expected to be found out.

"Men who lie are snakes," Cha'nel said angrily. "My husband is dead because of your deceit, and you along with your lap dog will pay for it," she finished with finality.

Terror knew that bargaining for his life was pointless, but if truth be told, he was ready to join his family in the afterlife. Living with the guilt of failing to protect his family was eating him up inside and for that failure, he felt he deserved death. But he had to make sure that Chaka got what she deserved before he left this earth. "Mem will tell ye wat'eva mem know about Chaka, but mem need ye ta promise mem one ting."

"What's that?" Cha'nel asked curiously. She could tell that he had accepted his fate, so she didn't see any harm in hearing him out.

"Make sure ye put 'er down," Terror said seriously. "Burn 'er and spread she ashes to the wind," he added to make sure she didn't hunt him in the afterlife.

"She's already dead, but she doesn't know it yet," Cha'nel said with a growl.

Terror didn't think it would be as easy as she was making it seem, but he kept his skepticism to himself and told her everything he knew about Chaka. Then he died.

King Killa 2

# CHAPTER 5

Sincere was watching the news report about Club 305 burning down to the ground last night and knew that his instincts were on point. He turned the volume on the television up just as the fire chief reported that the fire was definitely a case of arson.

They also reported that three bodies were found burned beyond recognition and would have to be identified through dental records. He knew that two of the bodies were Jay Jay and Charlene, but who was the third corpse? The only answer he could come up with was Mike Billy. That would explain why he wasn't getting an answer when he called him.

Bobby Lloyd had contacted him earlier that week and informed him that it was time to pull back the curtain on his fake death and expose Charlene, but Shinah showing up along with his sons threw a wrench in those plans. Shinah showing up had to be a coincidence because she thought her father was dead, a point made all the more real by the fact that she would have murdered him if Bobby wouldn't have made his presence known when he did. Seeing her after all this time let him know that he still loved her the same as the day she left, and that stripped him of the little control he had left. Over the years he had reached heights in the dope game that only a few were able to see, and most of them were memories - either behind the wall or six feet underground. But he couldn't have reached those heights without Charlene or Bobby: Charlene because she held the keys to the plug and Bobby because every move he made, he did so with is blessing. So he wasn't really in control of his situation, despite reaping the rewards. Most hustlers would be content to have unlimited money and power no matter who was pulling the strings, but not him. He considered himself a self-made man and he needed to be in control, so he kept himself from loving. He became cold and ruthless because that was the only thing he could control. Over the years there had been hundreds of women, and rarely did one make it past a week in his presence, but seeing Shinah again shattered that illusion because after twenty plus years, she still had a hold on hm. He hadn't heard from her or Bobby since they parted ways, but he knew they would be at the meeting he had called. He didn't know what was in store for him, but he would be ready for whatever.

\*\*\*

Chaka was back in Miami and she had an urgent need to go see Majestic. It was like a switch had been flipped inside of her after she had found out that Terror had betrayed her. Before, she had looked at Majestic strictly as a target because when she was on a job, she kept her emotions compartmentalized so as not to confuse things, but she could no longer deny the magnetic attraction she felt towards the young lion. As soon as she allowed herself to be a woman who liked a man instead of an assassin with a target, her emotions took control of her body and let her know that she was more than a little infatuated with him, which was dangerous in her line of work. But for the first time in a very long time, she wasn't working with that thought in mind. The urge to see the young lion suddenly became overwhelming, so she turned her rental around and headed to their family restaurant. She was hungry, but for more than just food.

\*\*\*

Shinah and her father were sitting in the kitchen, watching the news report about Club 305 being burned to the ground last night.

Finally Bobby had enough and turned the television off. He looked over at his daughter with a worried expression on his face and wondered if she knew how deep the water goes.

"What do you know, Daddy?" she asked quietly when she noticed his expression.

"More than you," he said sadly because he never intended for his daughter to know anything outside of rainbows and unicorns. But it seemed as if she had inadvertently married into the darkness that had permeated his life for longer than he could count. He wished he could bring Charlene back to life and murder her again, but he knew that he had to accept his share of the blame also because he could've done more. He was so caught up in making money that he put profits before his only child when she needed him the most. He turned to face her with every ounce of regret in his body showing in his eyes and told her, "I'm so, so sorry, baby."

Before Shinah could get him to explain what he was sorry for, she heard the patter of little feet running towards the kitchen and knew that her daughter was about to enter. "What did I tell you about running in the house?" she asked when she rounded the corner.

Gifted stopped suddenly when she spotted her mother and grandfather sitting at the breakfast nook. Before doing anything, she turned to her mother and responded to her question. "You said that running in the house was very dangerous and that it wasn't very ladylike." She repeated every word her mother told her about running in the house verbatim and smiled.

Shinah simply laughed because her daughter never ceased to amazon her.

Bobby also smiled at his granddaughter because she was very precocious.

"How are you today, Papa?" Gifted asked as she smiled at her grandfather. She, for one, acted like he had been around her whole life whereas her brother acted like he was a threat to his existence. "I'm good, sweetheart." He pulled her up into his lap. "How are you today?" he asked curiously.

"Oh, I'm excited to meet my new brothers today," she answered truthfully. She picked up a piece of fruit and started eating it, unaware of the impact her statement just made on the room.

Bobby looked over his granddaughter's head at his daughter with an arched eyebrow, wondering how she was going to handle the storm he foresaw on the horizon.

Shinah caught his look and sighed because she knew it was about to hit the fan. When she arrived home with her father in tow, she sat her husband and children down to explain everything that had transpired along with the consequences and repercussions of what those reactions might bring. She never hid anything from her family because she wanted them to be ready for any outcome, good or bad. She also thought about the reactions her sons would have towards her having a family when she never came to get them. She could pretty much guess Sincere's reaction, but she just hoped she was given the opportunity to explain everything before things went left.

She looked up when her son and husband walked into the kitchen together with matching scowls. She watched as Moosa's mind worked through everything she had told him. She knew that he would have the hardest time of her children because he took pride in being the big brother and all of sudden, he had not one, not two, but four big brothers over him. Her husband, on the other hand, did not have a problem with her sons. His issue was solely with Sincere. He knew how she felt about him, but he was content to let it be because he knew that she had planned on killing him for murdering her father. But when she showed up with her father in the flesh, he knew that things had changed, and he didn't know if he would be considered the winner when the dust settled.

Before they went to sleep, he fucked her. There was no other way to explain how he manhandled her body. It was rough and animalistic, but she didn't complain because she knew that he was trying to mark not only her body, but also her heart, and she almost felt that she deserved to be punished for the mess she had made of everything - almost! She looked his way and saw the apology in his eyes because he knew her better than most. He knew she was pissed and didn't know how she would let her anger show, but unbeknownst to him she had already forgiven him because she had a feeling that she would end up hurting him a lot worse in the end.

***

Majestic felt his anxiousness reach an alltime high when his family's restaurant came into view. He knew that he took his anger out on his sisters last night when he found out about the adoption and they didn't deserve that. It wasn't like they knew and kept it from him. So he knew that he needed to make it right. Despite everything, they were his family, if not by blood, then by deed, because they had held him down in ways that most wouldn't since he had been in Miami. He would make sure they never doubted how he felt about them ever again. He parked his car and stood for a few minutes watching his surroundings because he didn't forget that he was the leader of the Rude Boys despite the blessings his brother had bestowed upon him. He was raised out of the mud and he would never become comfortable enough to turn into a target.

After reassuring himself that all was well, he tucked his gun into the small of his back and made his way to make amends with the family he trusted the most.

\*\*\*

Chaka knew exactly when Majestic walked into the restaurant because he had an aura that made one uniquely aware of his presence. She watched him and smirked because she noticed things about him that most probably wouldn't even register, but she was trained to spot the subtleties. He didn't look as hungry as he did a few days ago, but it was still lurking beneath the surface, as if he was afraid to get comfortable with his newfound wealth. The designers he was wearing for his body fit perfectly, but she could tell that he was uncomfortable with the attention they were bringing him. Her trained eyes caught the hint of muscle moving beneath the expertly tailored clothes and she found her mind wondering what he looked like naked.

Majestic instantly felt uncomfortable when he walked in and saw the attention he was getting from staff and patrons alike. He was used to getting fearful glances from people who populated his family's restaurant, even though he was one of the owners, but now he was receiving appreciative glances from the women and nods of respect from the men. Mega, who was usually in the wind whenever he was around, gave him a head nod before going back to what he was doing. He knew that the only thing different about him was what he was wearing and he thought back to what King said about clothes being able to light your way if worn right. He was seeing firsthand the truth of that statement.

He started to head back to the office where he knew his sisters would be when he felt eyes on him. He looked around until he spotted the dark-skinned woman with the locs staring at him with a smirk ghosting around her lips. He locked eyes with her, fully expecting her to turn away, but was surprised when she smiled and arched an eyebrow. Intrigued, he studied her and realized that she was beautiful, but he sensed that she was much more than he looks. He felt drawn to her and started to go over to her until he heard his name being called.

He looked back and saw his sister Sky standing there with a vulnerability cloaking her arms that broke his heart because he knew that he was the cause of that. He went to her instantly, temporarily forgetting the woman who had captured his attention, but something compelled him to look back at her to see what he thought was a look of disappointment on her face. But it was gone so fast he thought that he might've imagined it.

Then he was in the office with his sisters and his mind was on the task at hand: fixing his family.

## CHAPTER 6

Latoya was sitting in the office, enjoying some quiet time alone with a nice cup of coffee before she was scheduled to appear in court later on that morning. She was perusing the newspapers on her laptop when a notice came through altering her that there was an article related to an earlier search she had conducted. She was about to ignore it when she noticed the names of Marco Perez and Sophia Gomez. She knew that King wouldn't be able to accept their betrayal, but she also knew that he wouldn't tell her anything pertaining to the citation and to tell the truth, she wanted it that way. So she had her computer set up to alert her if any news articles relating to Marco or Sophia popped up because she knew that the only newsworthy things those two would ever do would be getting locked up or dying, and since King was home, it would more than likely be the latter.

With that thought in mind, she clicked on the icon and saw that there were actually two articles. She tapped one and read about how Marco was found sitting in his car in traffic with two holes in his face. They chalked his murder up to revenge and she wondered if they knew how correct they were. She read Sophia's article and saw that she was killed in the shower, apparently during a home invasion. She didn't know how she felt about their deaths, but she knew without a doubt that King was the cause of them and she told him that she was with him through whatever. So she texted him the links to the articles and moved onto the next article about shady politics.

As she took another sip of her coffee they were no longer on her mind. Their fifteen minutes of fame were up.

\*\*\*

King heard the notification on his phone alerting him that he had an incoming text message. He looked and saw that wife had sent him a link to a website followed by her telling him that she loved him forever. He clicked on the link and saw the article pertaining to the murders of Marco Perez and Sophia Gomes. He erased the links from his phone and started to call Latoya, but decided to send a text instead. He didn't want to have that conversation on the phone because you never knew who might be listening in. After sending the message, he turned his attention back to Tango, who was staring at him like he had four heads, and in truth, he did, if you included his newfound brothers.

"Yo son, how did you get so fucking lucky?" Tango asked incredulously. After hearing the story, he was looking at King like he was a movie star. Hell, shit like this only happened in Hollywood.

King chuckled and looked at his comrade. He knew that money didn't change you per se. It changed the people around you. So he studied Tango because the moves he was about to make didn't leave room for error and he couldn't afford to have any question about anyone on his team. Going back to prison wasn't an option and anyone who moved funny, putting his freedom in question, would be taken off of the board. "Son, we were up, but the type of money we about to touch will put a different type of target on our backs," he said with a smirk gracing his lips. "We're about to be playing a whole different game with a different set of rules. No more block shit, no more hand to hand. You ready?" he asked cryptically.

Tango looked up at King suddenly when he heard the tone of his voice. I know this nigga not questioning my G, he thought angrily. "We are solid, but never imply in any way I'm not built for whatever is coming, because only a sucka would not be able to adapt and accept the consequences that come with that," he said, steel lacing every word.

King just nodded his head like he expected that response and was satisfied with it. "Tie up your affairs, because we're back to the city tomorrow," he said over his shoulder, leaving to handle some business before attending the meeting his father had called.

Tango stared at the door for a few seconds after it closed behind King and wondered if they were really ready to play on this level. Whether or not they were ready wasn't really the issue. It was if they would live long enough to enjoy the fruits of their labor.

\*\*\*

Czar was sitting in the Mandarin he had upgraded to on his brothers suggestion with Dior and Bianca, listening to their incessant questions about his brothers and family, wondering how they expected him to answer when they wouldn't shut up. "How can I answer anything when you won't stop running yeh mouths?" he drawled in his N'awlins accent.   It was comical how they both stopped talking at the very same moment. The looks on their faces told him that they were highly offended, but they kept silent which surprised him.

"Now one at a time, and one question at a time," he warned when he saw Dior about to take off with that mouth.

Rolling her eyes, Dior figured out which question she wanted to ask first. "You seem to be accepting your new family pretty easily," she said curiously. She knew Czar like the back of her hand and the way he was acting and carrying on wasn't normal. "It's not strange finding out you have there more people who look exactly like you?" she asked. She couldn't imagine three more Diors in the world.  Czar thought about her questions and really was shocked at how easily he and his brothers were getting along, but it would be impossible to hate someone who was you, literally. "How could I not?" he asked rhetorically with a smirk. "They are me and I'm them. We have the same likes and dislikes. We have the same mannerisms, which are almost exact replicas except for our accents. Yeah, it's scary, but how can I deny the reflections I see when I look at them? The whole situation is crazy as far as my family is concerned, but I'm bred in N'awlins, straight out the wards, and I will never change up on those who raised me. Loyalty makes you family; blood makes you related." He finished that last sentence with direct eye contact for Dior.

Dior couldn't explain the feelings that were moving through her body as he looked at her. His stare was so intense that it made her emotional. "You're my family, boy, we're your family," she told him as she pointed to herself and Bianca. "We're always been down for you," she added with tears in her eyes.    Bianca nodded her agreement. Seeing her best friend, her sister, get so emotional had her tearing up.

"I know, and that's why I'm going to take care of you," Czar said sincerely. He knew that he would need people in his life that wouldn't let him forget where he came from. "That dancing shit over," he added sternly. He wouldn't have his woman shaking her ass for a bunch of niggas.

"Done," Dior said simply. She was tired of that shit anyway.

Bianca looked at her and rolled her eyes in playful disgust. "Soft-ass bitch." She turned to Czar. "Who said I wanted to stop dancing?" she asked with an arched eyebrow.

"Why dance when you can own the club they are dancing in?" Czar asked seriously. He knew a woman of Bianca's caliber, someone used to making her own money, wouldn't be content eating off somebody and not earning her own. "Better yet, I'll buy you a club," he added with a smirk.

"Boy, you don't have to lie to me. We ain't fucking," she replied with an eye roll.

"Li'l boys lie," Czar said as he stood up to finish getting dressed for the family meeting in a few hours. He was looking forward to seeing his brothers again. "Men tell the truth regardless of the consequences. If I said it, then that's what it is," he added seriously.

"We're going to fuck around and be sister wives if he buy me a club," she playfully said to Dior.

Dior rolled her eyes before turning to Czar, who was ready to go. "What time will you be back?" she asked quietly.

"No telling," he replied as he looked at her.

"This is all still so new, so we'll see. I'll call and let you know," he added as he walked towards the door.

"Okay," she answered as he opened the door. "I love you!" she called out desperately before he walked out.

"I know you do," he called out over his shoulder before closing the door behind him.

"Girl, you know he loves you," Bianca told her best friend when she saw the look of despair on her face.

"I know, girl, but sometimes I need to hear it," Dior said sorrowfully.

Czar was standing in the hallway with the door cracked, listening to Dior and Bianca. Hearing the pain in Dior's voice made him want to go back in and comfort her, but then he grew angry because his actions spoke loud and clear. If that wasn't enough, then so be it, he thought as he silently shut the door and walked off.

*** 

Chaka was walking through the lobby of her hotel, distracted because her mind was still on the young lion. She was a little disappointed that he didn't approach her, but it didn't faze her in the least because she knew that time was on her side. She was digging through her purse searching for her room key when she collided with a solid body. Instinctively, she dropped her purse and grabbed onto the man to negate any advantage he might've given him by being distracted. She suddenly remembered that she was playing a role and immediately released him and backed up. She looked up at him and felt a smile form on her face. Standing in front of her, looking better than he did at his restaurant, was her young lion. As she studied him she frowned, because his energy was different. Something was wrong, and as soon as he opened his mouth, she knew that she was straight.

"Excuse me, ma," King said as he bent down to pick up his phone and her purse. He stood back up and handed her the purse back. "I apologize because I was locked onto my phone and not paying attention to where I was going," he added with a polite smile.

Chaka felt her pussy throb when he smiled at her, but she was confused. Here standing in front of her was her young lion, but he wasn't her young lion. He looked exactly like him, but his whole energy was different. She pegged his accent from New York City and his swagger matched perfectly. At first she thought that he was trying to trick her, but the more she studied him, the more she knew that it was natural and not an illusion. That left only one conclusion: this was the young lion's twin brother. "It's okay," she replied with a smile of her own, "Mem dinna look where mem twas going either," she added as she accepted her purse from him.

King was captivated by her accent, then he took a second to really look at her and realized that she was drop dead gorgeous. "Apologies again for my rudeness," he said as he extended his hand. "My name is King, Miss…?"

Chaka broke out in her natural smile because he thought he was smooth, and in truth, he was. "Chaka; my name is Chaka," she told him as she shook his hand.

"Well, it was nice meeting you, Miss Chaka," King told her before walking off.

Chaka watched him walk off with a thoughtful expression on her face. She never liked an unanswered question and with that on her mind, she followed behind him. Before she exited the hotel lobby, she looked down at the purse in her hand in disgust and threw it in the trash. Nobody had to know that it cost ten thousand dollars.

## CHAPTER 7

"You think this is a good idea?" Bobby asked his daughter as they rode to the meet with Sincere.

Shinah just looked at her father silently because she had nothing else to say about the matter. They had been over this already and her mind was made up. Whether it was a good idea or not, it had to be done.

Bobby just sighed because he didn't know if she was being naive, stubborn, or both. Either way, he knew that he would stand with her, right or wrong.

"Don't worry Papa," Gifted said as she laid her hand into his. "Everything will be okay." She sounded so optimistic it brought a smile to his face. Moosa snorted in disgust, but kept his silence. Regardless of how he felt, he would keep it to himself because he didn't want to disrespect his mother. He would just let everything play out.

Shinah looked at her son and felt his pain, but she didn't speak about it. He would have to deal with this like the man they were teaching him to be. She glanced at her husband and felt his energy emanating from him in waves. He was the wild card because Sincere was his weakness and they had never met. She just hoped he kept his peace because if he didn't, it could go left, and there was nothing she could do about it if it did. She smiled at her daughter because she would be her greatest creation, but her smile didn't reach her eyes. She knew her four sons would feel some type of way, but they were the least of her worries. Sincere would see this as the ultimate betrayal despite her not knowing the truth behind his actions twenty-five years ago. After her father told her all of the details behind his fake death, she felt even worse because Sincere was trapped, yes by his own greed, but also by his love for her. Her father said that the only reason he agreed to do it was to protect her and she never believed in his love enough to seek out the truth from him. She ran and vowed revenge, revenge that had been eating her from the inside out and now she didn't know if it was too late, but she would find out soon enough.

When she felt the SUV slow to a stop at their destination, she looked up to find her husband's gaze like he could see her feelings. She looked away and slid out of the SUV. She took a deep breath to regain her composure because she couldn't afford any slip-ups. This meeting would change all of their lives - literally.

***

Sincere put the phone down after being informed that Shinah and her entourage had arrived. He had been up all day preparing for this meeting and wondering what he would say to her the next time he saw her. He knew that Bobby probably gave her the truth behind his actions twenty-five years ago. The same truth he had planned on telling her when he returned to the hospital but she is gone. Now everything would be laid bare and what will be, will be. He made sure that everyone involved knew that the meeting was weapon free because he couldn't afford for the scene in the V.I.P. room to repeat itself. Even though he had rented out the whole floor beneath the penthouse, he knew the reports of gunshots at the hotel would get the appropriate response from the authorities and no matter who he had on his payroll, it would be an untenable situation to get out of.

He looked at the Royal Oak Offshore Audemers Peugeot timepiece on his wrist and made his way over to the elevator that opened into a sitting area of the penthouse. It wasn't lost on him that he was dealing with another elevator that would deliver him more surprises that he had to deal with. Once he saw the numbers rising towards his position, he prepared himself for whatever happened next.

Shinah led her group into the hotel lobby as she tried to conceal her nervousness. She felt a tug on her hand and smiled down at her daughter, who was bubbling with excitement at meeting her brothers. "What is it, baby?" she asked sweetly.

"I was just trying to slow you down, Mommy, because you were starting to drag me a little," Gifted said teasingly as her smile grew.

Despite herself, Shinah laughed. Her daughter had a way of slowing her down, so she did just that. She took a deep breath and discreetly studied her surroundings. She immediately noticed the extra muscle situated around the lobby trying to blend in. They weren't obvious, but to a trained eye like hers, they stuck out like black men at a Klan rally. She looked at her husband and father and saw that they noticed them also. She understood why Sincere wanted the meeting weapon free considering what happened at the club, but to see all of this manpower reminded her that he wouldn't be completely defenseless. She also knew that her husband had his men a few blocks away, ready to swoop in and save them if he pressed the button she knew he had somewhere on his body.

She glanced at her father once again to see him staring at him. She saw the many questions in his eyes but she knew he would keep them to himself because she had let him know in no uncertain terms that she was doing this her way. She took another deep breath and headed for the elevator that would take them to the penthouse. She could feel eyes tracking their progress, but they were ignored. Once inside, she pressed the appropriate button and felt her heart rate quicken.

\*\*\*

Sincere didn't realize that he was holding his breath as he watched the numbers get closer and closer to his position until he was forced to breathe. He couldn't believe how nervous he was about seeing Shinah again when it had only been less than a day since their last encounter, but he was, and this time she wouldn't catch him by surprise - not when he was ready for her. He checked his outfit again to make sure he was wrinkle and lint free. He wanted to look perfect. He straightened up just as the doors to the elevator opened up. His smile naturally broke out when he saw her, but instantly disappeared when he noticed the little girl she was leading by the hand as she walked towards him. He was stuck in quicksand. So much for being ready for her, he thought in dismay.

It seemed as if the elevator was taking forever to reach their destination but in reality, it was only seconds before the doors opened and she saw him standing there looking debonair. She felt hope when she saw him smile, but it disappeared just as fast when his eyes landed on someone else. At first she thought it might've been her husband's energy that drew his attention, but when she followed his eyes, she saw that he was focused on her daughter. She saw the myriad of emotions playing across his face as he connected the dots and it hurt her heart more than she could express at that moment to see the betrayal and hurt in his eyes. He quickly covered them with a smirk, but she saw through the facade. He was in pain. She stopped a few feet away and waited for him to speak, since it was his meeting. When she saw that he had no intention of easing, the tension she decided to make the proper introductions.

"Sincere, this is——"

"Your daughter," he said just above a whisper. Anyone could see that the little girl was Shinah's twin in every way. He looked to Bobby for some type of answer or clue, but all he got from the stoic old man was sadness and disappointment. Another setback in the line of many, he thought seriously as he nodded for her to continue her introductions.

Shinah just nodded and got on with it. "This is my son Moosa." She pointed at the gangly teenager, who was scowling at Sincere. He didn't even know what the problem with him was, but he knew that his father didn't like him, and that was enough for him. "And this is---"

"Her husband," Moses growled loudly. It was obvious to all present that he was staking his claim, marking his territory.

Shinah grimaced and rolled her eyes at her husband's childish buffoonery, but she held her tongue. She would deal with him in private.

Sincere was confused at the aggression and animosity he felt washing over him from a man he was a hundred percent certain he had never met or heard of before this very moment. He glanced at Bobby and received the signal that all would be revealed later, then he looked at Shinah, who refused to meet his eyes. Then, like a bolt of lightning it hit him. This man was jealous of him. He hadn't seen or heard from Shinah in over two decades so the only reason he had for feeling like he was, was because she gave him a reason to do so. If his reaction was any indication, then she gave him a real big reason to feel as insecure as he was acting. Back in control, he just smirked at the man who was hyperventilating like a bull ready to charge.

Shinah grabbed her husband's arm and walked him a few feet away before having a whispered conversation that seemed to calm him down considerably. "Sorry about that," she said when they walked back over. "I wanted to explain some things——" she started to say before Sincere cut her off.

"Save it for when our sons get here. Besides, I'm sure they will love to hear about your family," he told her sarcastically before walking to the bar to fix himself a drink.

Shinah watched him walk off with a frown on her face because he was still as irritating as he was so many years ago. But he was right. Their sons were a different story altogether. She looked down at her daughter, who was tugging on her hand again. "Yes, baby?" "Are my brothers coming?" Gifted asked hopefully. Shinah smiled at her daughter because de- spite the tension, she was locked in on meeting her brothers. Her innocence was pure and she would protect it at all costs. "Yes, baby, they are coming."

Happy at her answer, Gifted released her hand and skipped over to where her brother and father were sitting.

"I hope that you know what you're doing, baby," Bobby whispered into her ear when he walked over and wrapped his arm around her shoulders.

Shinah sighed as she leaned into his em- brace. She had a feeling that she was going to need all of the strength she could get. She looked over at Sincere, who was staring at her with an intense look on his face. Moses's childish display of dominance revealed some cards she didn't want known at the moment, especially not to Sincere, and made himself look like the lesser man. She felt her husband glaring at her, but she refused to acknowledge him. She sighed again and sent up a prayer for guidance. She glanced up at her father and rolled her eyes when she saw him smirking at her. "I hope I know what I'm doing too." Because if I don't, a lot of people will get hurt, she thought sadly.

**CHAPTER 8**

Chaka was flabbergasted by what she had seen. She had followed her young lion to the Four Seasons hotel across town and at first, nothing out of the ordinary happened, but then she spotted the hired muscle posted up in strategic positions around the hotel. She saw by the movements that they were professional. They were obvious to her because she was trained to spot things like that, but to an ordinary person, they would look like they belonged. The extra security had her wondering what her young lion was into and it also piqued her professional curiosity. So she sat low and waited to see what happened next.

She didn't have long to wait because she saw her young lion pull up and get out the back of a taxi. She knew it was him because she felt his energy. He screamed sophisticated rudeness whereas his twin was more city cool. She waited until he was inside the hotel before she got out of the rental car she was driving while in town, but before she crossed the street, two black SUVs rolled into the valet circle. A security team was out of the trucks in seconds, securing the perimeter for whoever was still inside. She was now ultra aware of her surroundings because something was happening that she was not aware of, and in her business, not knowing could get you killed. She saw that the hired muscle around the hotel were also aware, but making no sudden movements, as if they were expecting high profile people to be attending whatever was happened in the hotel. She was sure that pictures were being taken of every car, truck, and SUV entering the valet along with the people coming and going, so she casually retreated back to her rental car. But she didn't leave because she wanted - no, she needed - to see what her young lion was up to.

She watched as who she assumed was the boss in need of the security team step out of the back of the SUV and felt her heart skip a best as she realized that her young lion had two identical brothers.

No, make that three identical brothers, she thought, astonished, as another man stepped out of the SUV who mirrored her young lion. Now that she was aware that there were four of them, she noticed the subtle differences. They were minute, but they were there if you knew to look for them.

She thought about going into the hotel, but decided against it. She didn't want to take the chance of being recognized by her young lion or his brother. Plus, she didn't want her picture taken. That would be bad for business. She got comfortable because she didn't plan on leaving until she absolutely had to.

***

Pharaoh and Czar were enjoying each other's company as they rode to the family meeting together. Czar had called Pharaoh to come get him because he didn't want to catch a cab or Uber. It was strange how comfortable he was with his brothers already, especially after the betrayal of Jimmy Slim, but not trusting them never once crossed his mind because it would be like not trusting himself.

"So what do you expect from this meeting?" Pharaoh asked, snapping him out of his reverie.

Czar thought about his question and really didn't know what to expect. "Honestly, I don't know what to expect because all of this is crazy," he answered truthfully. Over the last few weeks, he had been fighting his livelihood, catching bodies all over the south, but that seemed like another life now.

Pharaoh nodded like he expected that answer. He thought about how much his life had changed since his graduation. Three people were assassinated in the auditorium that day, he thought angrily, my mother, my father, and my old self.

"You good?" Czar asked, seeing the emotion flit across his face.

"Yeah, yeah," Pharaoh answered, shaking his head. "I never expected any of this. My birth father is responsible for my adoptive parents' deaths directly and indirectly. Our birth mother been M.I.A. for our whole lives. It's just a lot to take in," he said, perplexed at how much has happened in the last year.

Czar was nodding in agreement before he even finished because he felt the exact same way. "All this is too coincidental to me," he said seriously. He was a street thoroughbred and if it was too good to be true, then it usually was. "We've never met before or even had any clue about each other, but we all ended up in the same club at the same time. Us, our brothers, our pops, our mama, our grandparents, all in the same room at the same time after never meeting in our lives," he finished skeptically. "Definitely something underhanded is

afoot." Pharaoh seriously doubted that fate had anything to do with it. Somebody was pulling a lot of strings.

"Afoot?" Czar repeated with smirk. "Bro, you need to cut all of that college shit out," he added with a laugh.

Pharaoh tried to hold his serious face, but the laughter was contagious and he joined his brother. It felt good to release some of the tension they both were feeling ahead of the meeting. He felt his phone vibrating and pulled it out to see that he had a text from King. "Our brothers are waiting for us in the lobby. He said there's extra security everywhere." He looked up at Czar with a smirk on his face. "I guess they don't want a repeat of last night."

Czar nodded. "Most definitely why this meeting was called without arms." He felt naked without his grave diggers on him.

"We're here," Pharaoh announced when he felt them pull to a stop.

Czar grabbed the door handle, ready to get out, when he felt Pharaoh grabbed his arm. He looked back with a question in his eyes.

"Wait a second." Pharaoh knew how serious Lion took his job of protecting him and didn't want this chief protector upset with him again for not following his directions.

Czar wasn't used to the bodyguard shit, but he waited until he realized that he was playing in a different league now. He vowed to never rely on another man to save his life when he was built for that action. The minute you got comfortable was the minute you got fitted for a casket.

"We're good, boss," Lion said as he opened the door for Pharaoh, who nodded and stepped out of the SUV followed by Czar. "Are you ready to see what afoot is?" Pharaoh asked with a smile.

"As I'll ever be," Czar responded with a smile of his own.

They walked into the hotel surrounded by Lion and his security team. In a town used to seeing celebrities, they had people on high alert, trying to see who was behind the wall of muscle and get a picture, but they were bigger than any rapper or reality television star. They just didn't know it yet.

"Lion, you will come up with me and my brothers," Pharaoh ordered when he spotted King and Majestic waiting on them. "The rest of the team can post up wherever it seems proper."

Lion nodded once he received his orders and set about carrying them out to the letter. "You two walked in here like movie stars," King joked as he greeted his brothers.

"You didn't see the movie Four Brothers?" Czar joked. "It's about us."

"Bruddas," Majestic greeted warily. He was excited to see his brothers again, but he felt naked without his guns. "You good?" Czar asked him as he recog- nized the look in his brother's eyes

Majestic locked eyes with him and nodded. "Well, let's get this show on the road," King said as he led the way to the elevators once Lion rejoined them.

The elevator was quiet as they rode up because everyone was lost in their own thoughts. The unknown was looming, but it was too late to turn back now. Whatever happened, they would face it together. They had each other now and nothing would tear that apart.

***

Sincere hung the phone up and looked at Shinah. "Our sons are on the way up," he stated simply, like those words didn't hold a weight all of their own.

Shinah nodded and stood up. She hoped her sons understood why she did the things she did, but she knew from personal experience that things rarely went the way you wanted them to.

"Mommy, is that my brothers coming up?" Gifted asked excitedly.

"Yes, baby, it's them." Shinah answered her daughter, but her eyes were on her son, Moosa. She could tell that he was upset by the excitement that his sister was displaying for some brothers she had never formally met before. He felt like he was no longer important in her life and he resented that. She made a mental note to have a talk with him soon.

She looked up at the numbers above the elevator and felt herself growing more anxious the closer they got to her position. She was suddenly aware of someone standing beside her and looked up to find Sincere shoulder to shoulder with her, giving her support like he had always done from the moment he met her. She promised to make it up to him, but right now, she had another obstacle to get over. One problem at a time, she thought. She breathed a sigh of relief when the elevator opened up and she saw her children healthy and whole. She remembered everything she had went through to get them to this world and thanked God that she had them. She looked at her four identical grown sons and suddenly felt her age. Just looking at them, you couldn't tell them apart, but she knew her children even though she hadn't been in their lives. "King, Czar, Majestic and Pharaoh" she called out, pointing to each of them in turn.

Surprise lit all of their faces as she remembered their names, but they kept it in check as they stepped off the elevator and approached their birth parents.

"I'm impressed," King whispered in her ear before kissing her cheek.

By the time she finished hugging and greeting her sons, she was crying. She was just overwhelmed by emotion because of the reception she was receiving. She looked over and saw Sincere staring at his sons with an awkward expression on his face. She laughed at him. She couldn't help it.

She had never seen him like this before and it was cute.

Sincere frowned at her because he knew that she was laughing at him. He was looking at the men he saw before him. It pissed him off and saddened him all at the same time.

King looked at each one of his brothers and gave them the nod to follow his lead.

Sincere's saw his sons crowd him and tensed up, not because he was scared, but because he was fearful that they were going to hug him and start getting emotional. That, he definitely wasn't ready for.

"So, you're our father?" King asked seriously.

"Why are you tensing up like we're about to hug you, old man?" Czar asked with a smirk

Sincere looked each of his sons in their eyes and smirked because the move they had pulled by getting in his personal space was something he used to do when he was younger to make people uncomfortable. His bloodline was alive and well.

"Whose genes do you think is the most dominant in our blood?" Pharaoh asked his brothers.

"Our mudda," Majestic said seriously, but he had a little twinkle in his eyes that told everyone he was enjoying himself.

"Definitely our mother," Pharaoh agreed. "Did y'all see her pop her own mother and was getting ready to pop our father before some weird shit started happening?" King chimed in amusingly. "Seriously though, we all know you weren't in our lives by force and not by choice. So we don't blame you for circumstances out of your control." King made sure he was looking his father in his eyes when he said that because he wanted him to see that he meant every word.

"Yeah, despite the shit we've all been through, we came out of the fine still intact. We're all thoroughbreds," Czar added. "You have four good ones in us. Your bloodline is presented real well."

Majestic nodded his head in agreement. He wasn't a man of many words, but he knew he was standing in front of them.

"Aww, isn't this sweet."

Everyone turned to look at Moosa, who was glaring at the four brothers. It was deja vu all over again.

"What's with all of the heat coming from over there?" Czar asked Sincere as he noticed the young boy standing beside a bigger version of himself and both of them shooting daggers their way with their eyes.

Sincere wanted to see Shinah in the hot seat, but as he looked at the worried expression on her face, his first instinct was to step in and help her. But then he realized that he couldn't do anything to help her untangle the web she had them all stuck in. This was her mess to clean up and hers alone. "That's a question for your mother," he replied diplomatically

Shinah looked at Moosa and sighed because a fire had started. She only had herself to blame for that because she taught him to meet any problems head on, and right now, he saw her older sons as a problem he needed to meet. She looked at her husband and knew that he wouldn't be any help. Secretly she felt like he wanted Moosa to start a confrontation because he never would. Her husband was a spoiled man who was too used to his father's power and did not know how to react when things didn't go his way. She knew that they needed to get control of this situation and fast. She beckoned her daughter to her side and looked at her sons. "Czar, Majestic, Pharaoh, and King. I would like to introduce you to some people. Some very important people in my life." She was meeting each of their gazes because she was their mother and there would be no hiding. She owed them the full truth. "That's my husband, Moses Bandele of Nigeria. That's our son Moosa and this pretty young lady at my side is our daughter Gifted."

"What the fuck?" Czar whispered harshly. He couldn't believe his eyes. He couldn't believe that his birth mother had finally showed up in their lives after a quarter century and brought her family like shit was sweet. "You've got to be fucking kidding me with this shit," he growled. He couldn't control his rage at the sight in front of him. After the things he went through growing up, for her to show up with her family was a betrayal, plain and simple. He looked at his brothers and saw varying degrees

of emotion displayed on their faces, but none as strong as his own. He was alone on this. Fuck it, he thought angrily, I'm used to being by myself.

"You betta watch your mouth talking to my mother!" Moosa shouted as he stood by his mother and sister. His hand instinctively went to his waist where he usually kept his gun, but today it was empty due to the rules of the meeting.

Czar caught the move and smirked because now they were speaking his language. He was fluent in murder and spoke it frequently. "Young'un I have more bodies than you and your sister's combined ages," he spoke truthfully. "Stay in you lane and out of my business," he warned.

"Anything concerning these two," Moosa said, pointing to her mother and sister, "is my business. She has been my mother my whole life. You just met her yesterday," he said with a sneer.

## CHAPTER 9

The room was deathly silent following Moosa's last statement. Even Shinah didn't know what to say. Everything was crumbling around her. She looked at the room in dismay because there was an invisible line drawn as if a war was on the horizon. Sincere and their sons were on one side, she and her family aligned with her father were on the other. She didn't know what to do. The look on her firstborn's face told her that Moosa's comment had hit home, had made it real in a way it wasn't before. She was about to say something to try and regain control, but Czar beat her to it.

"You're right, little nigga, it was my choice to be put up for adoption, to grow up in the Ninth Ward with a voodoo priestess for a mother, to have her then go to prison when I was twelve, to rob and steal so I wouldn't starve, to have everything I ever loved washed away in Katrina, to have to kill to live, to be standing here in front of a woman who thought I was better off where I was while she was raising another family..." He didn't realize that he had tears in his eyes and even though he wouldn't let them fall, the emotion was all in his voice. "You're sitting here acting like you're a gangsta when everything's been handed to you. I'm a gangsta because I had to be in order to live. Nobody fed me but me. Nobody clothed me but me. Nobody protected me but me. I missed out knowing my brothers, my reflections, all because of choices made when I wasn't even talking yet. So you're right, young'un, she's your mother because she hasn't earned the right to be mine." As he said this last statement, he made sure he was looking Shinah in her eyes. Then and only then did he let a tear fall down his face.

Shinah sobbed as she heard the pain in her child's voice. She looked at her sons and couldn't imagine the horrors her decisions caused them to go through. She locked eyes with Sincere and was shocked to see tears in his eyes. It was at that moment she realized how wrong her choices were twenty-five years ago. Despite her feelings at the time, she should've put her children's needs before her own, and now it might be too late.

Sincere looked at the anguish on Shinah's face and knew that he couldn't let her carry this blame alone. He cleared his throat and looked at his sons. "Your mother is the best woman I know and I'm sure that she did what she thought was best at the time, but she's not to blame. I am." He finally realized that he was the domino that started it all. "Back then, I was all about my money and I was blinded by greed. I left her in her most vulnerable state. I was tasked with a mission to kill her father, but I couldn't, and he was expecting it either way. The only reason he didn't have me killed then was because Shinah was pregnant with you boys and I was the father. We came up with a plan together to expose Charlene, but Shinah was gone when I got back, so I couldn't explain it all to her. Can you imagine her thinking that everybody in her life she loved was lost to her? I know for a fact that she wouldn't have left you boys if she didn't think it was necessary. This thing is way deeper than any of you know and it's life and death, literally. Everything will be explained during this meeting, but we need to get this shit off of our chests because we don't have time for emotion when it gets thick. It will get you killed or the one you love killed. So don't just blame your mother. Blame me because I had a direct role in her leaving you." He took a deep breath and looked over at Shinah. The look of gratitude and love on her face shot straight to his heart, but he wasn't the only one who noticed it.

"Wife!" Moses shouted as he stood up. His face was balled up in anger because he knew that he was fighting a losing battle. "You have to choose," he demanded. His heavy accent gave his words a menacing tone.

"Father," Moosa tentatively called out. He had never heard his father talk to his mother in any way other than a loving tone.

"Silence, boy!" Moses shouted at his son, but his eyes never left Shinah's. "This is between your mother and me," he added.

Shinah looked at her husband and shook her head sadly. "Moses, this is not the time or place for this discussion," she said firmly.

Moses didn't miss the fact that she called him by his name and not husband, as was her custom since they had been married. That more than anything was the only answer he needed. "You came here to avenge your father by murdering the man who killed him." He realized that it was a moot point now, but he had no cards left to play.

Shinah almost pitied him, but things had changed, and he refused to see that. "He didn't kill my father, and that was the only thing I had against him. Ours was an arrangement of convenience and I upheld against him. Ours was an arrangement of convenience and I uphold my end of things." She motioned to their children. "Don't make this any harder than it needs to be," she cautioned seriously.

Moses frowned angrily because everyone was staring at him as she chastised him. He pressed the panic button in his pocket and smirked at her. Shinah looked at him confused as to what he was smirking about, then noticed his hand in pocket where she knew the panic button was located. She looked up and noticed his smirk had turned into a full-blown smile.

"You didn't," she said accusingly.

Before she could say anything further, she noticed the numbers on an elevator moving towards their position. "Moosa, you and your sister stand behind me," she told them frantically. She didn't know what to expect when those doors opened up, but she couldn't put anything past Moses in the state he was in. His jealousy was confusing to her because he already knew what it was, but he was moving out of control and that wasn't like him.

"What's going on, Shinah?" Sincere asked, picking up on her energy. He looked at her husband and saw that he was still focused on her.

"Take our boys and move over by the bar," she pleaded as she looked at him. "He had a panic button in his pocket in case things went south in this meeting, and he pressed it while we were talking." She was so angry at Moses she could barely look at him.

Sincere looked at Moses with a look of disgust as he walked over to another phone on his desk to call the head of his security team downstairs. He had a look of concern on his face when it kept ringing. He glanced at Moses again and saw that he was snow smirking at him. He put his phone down and walked over to the bar. He pressed a hidden button and watched the alcohol rack slide down to reveal enough artillery to wage war on a small country. "Czar, Majestic, King, and Pharaoh, come strap up," he told his sons as he grabbed a 9mm Beretta and made sure it had one in the head. He looked at Moses with a smirk of his own. "You have to get up real early in the morning to get over me."

Moses frowned and vowed to kill Sincere the first chance he got.

Czar grabbed the two forty-four Magnum revolvers he saw hanging in there, calling his name. He almost felt like he was getting ready to cheat on his grave diggers, but they looked so much alike that he couldn't help himself.

"If anything remotely resembling a threat steps off that elevator, dead it," Sincere said after he saw that his sons were armed and ready to go.

"Sincere, wait," Shinah pleaded. She knew that if she didn't gain control of the situation, it would go to a place there was no coming back from. "Just wait please." She needed him to hear her words.

Sincere looked at her and knew that she was still his greatest weakness. He nodded that he would wait and follow her lead.

"Moosa, where are you going?" she asked him when he started moving away from her. "To get me one of those guns," he said seriously. He didn't like being without arms when everyone else around him was strapped up.

"No!" she barked. "Get back over here now."

Moosa heard the tone of her voice and knew that she wasn't playing. Despite how uncomfortable he was, he did as she asked. He walked back to her side he looked up and frowned angrily when he noticed Czar smirking at him. He turned his head and bit his tongue.

Before anyone else could say anything, the elevator opened up and out walked a beautiful woman with blood red hair who looked almost exactly like Shinah. "Oh, I didn't miss the family reunion," she said sarcastically in her melodic voice as she took everyone in.

"Where is my man?" Moses growled angrily when he noticed that the elevator was empty of anyone except her. "Moses Bandele, son of Ahmad. Your men

are under my care for the time being," she said sardonically. The way she looked at him let everyone in the room know she didn't think much of him.

"On whose authority?" Moses shouted. He wanted to know who this woman was who thought she could commandeer his men without his authority. He decided everyone on his security detail would be executed immediately.

"On the authority of the Council, of course," she said seriously. She narrowed her eyes and dared him to question her further.

Moses was shocked into silence and knew that she was indeed powerful enough to do what she said. He also knew that his father was involved in some way, and that was even worse.

Shinah was staring at the woman in front of her, bewildered as to who she was. The way her husband all but kneeled to her spoke to how dangerous she was and that only succeeded in confusing her. She also couldn't help noticing a resemblance between them, but she had never seen the woman before, that much she was sure of.

"My name is Royalty Salvatore, but most people call me——"

"The red viper," Bobby said angrily. He knew that her presence spelled trouble for all of them.

"Ahhh, so my reputation precedes me. Although only my enemies call me the red viper," Royalty said enigmatically. "You're not my enemy, are you, Bobby Lloyd?" she asked seriously. Her face transformed so fast that it was easy so see why she was nicknamed after one of the deadliest snakes in the world.

"At least not yet," Bobby answered mysteriously.

Royalty eyed him for a long moment as if to access his threat level. Then she smirked and was sad. "You look really well for a dead man, Bobby Lloyd."

"Who are you?" Shinah asked emphatically before her father could say anything else. She was starting to get a strange feeling in her gut and she needed answers.

"Since you know who I am, then you obviously know what I'm capable of," Royalty said, ignoring Shinah as she continued to address Bobby. "Your presence has been duly noted by the powers to be, but we'll address your indiscretions at a later date," she said cryptically. "Have you told her yet?" she asked seriously.

Bobby knew that his house of cards was on the verge of collapse and there was nothing he could do to stop it.

"Tell me what?" Shinah asked with a hint of desperation in her voice. "Tell me what, Daddy?" she screamed when no one answered her.

"I'm so, so sorry, baby," Bobby said quietly as he avoided her eyes.

Sincere was watching the scene play out in front of him and knew that Pandora's box was about to be opened. He gave his sons a look that said be on point.

Royalty looked at Bobby in disgust. "Silly playing the coward, Bobby." She sneered at him. "Bobby Lloyd is not your father," she said, finally addressing Shinah directly.

"Oh shit," Sincere mumbled to himself. "What!" Shinah shroud as the implications of what she just said to her sank in. "Tell me she's lying!" She looked at Bobby with fury bleeding from every pore.

Bobby looked angrily at Royalty before turning to Shinah. "Let me explain," he said calmly. He never wanted to hurt her, but it seemed as if that's all he'd done directly and indirectly with his actions.

"Tell me she's lying!" Shinah spat each word forcefully. She gave up her children to avenge this man, and now she was finding out that he wasn't even her father.

"I can't tell you that," Bobby said quietly. The realization that her whole life was a lie was just too much for her to take. She walked over to Bobby and smacked him across his face. "I abandoned my sons for you, to avenge you, and it was all a lie. I will never forgive you and I will never speak to you again." Shinah couldn't believe what was happening to her. No one could imagine what she had been through the last twenty-five years, and it was all for nothing. The man she had walked through hell and back for wasn't even her father. She turned to her sons and hated herself for what she did to them. She would spend the rest of her life making it right if they let her.

"We forgive you," King told her before she could say anything. He hadn't spoken to any of his brothers, but it felt right. They realized how she had been manipulated by the circumstances of her life and they had much bigger things going on than to hold a grudge.

Shinah was overwhelmed with emotions as she looked at each one of her sons and saw that they all felt the same way, even Czar. It was a start, but she knew that she had a long way to go.

"That's sweet," Royalty said sarcastically. She was really jealous because she was never allowed to have kids of her own. Not that she wanted any because in her line of work, they were liabilities that could get you killed. She should know because she had gotten to a few of her targets through their progeny.

Shinah bristled in anger, but she kept her composure as she faced Royalty. "I'm assuming we share the same father," she said seriously.

Royalty studied Shinah and wasn't that impressed with her. She had to admit that she was stronger than she thought, but that was to be expected given their bloodline. She was about to put into motion a series of moves that could get everyone in this room murdered, but if it all went well, then they would be untouchable. She smirked at Shinah and hoped she was worthy of the positon she was about to be placed in. "So, you're not just a pretty face after all," she said snidely. "Our father is a man by the name of Javier Salvatore. Our mother was murdered by one of your sons." She glanced over at her nephews, who were all staring at her and seemed to lose her train of thought. "Moses, I need you to remove yourself from this room. You're not family and this is bloodline business." She didn't even look at him as she ordered him from the room.

"What about my children?" he protested weakly.

Royalty just looked at him until he sighed heavily and left the room on the elevator. She looked at Moosa, who was staring at the elevator his father just disappeared into with a frown on his face. "Be glad that you have my bloodline inside of you also," she told him seriously.

Shinah glared at her, but she just shrugged it off. "Better he finds out early," she told her sister. Shinah's glare remained, but she didn't dispute her claims.

Royalty turned back to her nephews and glared. "Who is going to pay for my mother's murder?" she asked menacingly.

## CHAPTER 10

The room was eerily quiet until Majestic stepped forward with his gun gripped tightly in his hand. He wasn't raised to be a coward and could hold the weight for his deeds, whatever they were, but it would be a massacre before he laid down for anyone. "Mem put the snake down," he said in a tone that left no doubt he would do it again if it played out the same way.

Not even a second ticked by before Czar and King stepped up beside their brother. Pharaoh wasn't far behind. "If he is carrying the weight, then we are all toting some load," King said seriously. Words were meaningless where action was needed. Loyalty was bred through every fiber of his being and he let it show.

"Yeah, Auntie, let us know how this movie gonna play out," Czar said sarcastically. He was in. His nuts tightened up. He let him hang and let the bodies pile up. "I've always wanted to play Jason," he added with a smirk.

Royalty laughed despite herself. Their little display of loyalty impressed her because she knew that they just met less than twentyfour hours ago. She also found the one with the smart mouth amusing. "Your ignorance is amusing because you don't know any better. I belong to an organization that wouldn't blink before assassinating all four you despite your bravado and sarcasm." She let that marinate before continuing. "You're pawns, but you have the potential to be so much more. You ever wonder why all four of you were named the way you were?" she asked rhetorically. "Czar, King, Majestic and Pharaoh, all names of royalty, all powerful names. All to prepare you for the roles you would eventually play. You killed your grandmother, my mother, and didn't know that you removed a powerful piece from one side of the board. She was wicked, evil, even conniving. A master manipulator. But she was also brilliant.

She controlled some of the most powerful men in this world with a touch, a whisper, a promise or a look. She built a network on the back of these men. She made them think their every move was their own but in reality, was continued by her own machination. She corrupted every man she felt could advance her life except two: Bobby Lloyd and our father, Javier Salvatore. My father was in business with Bobby when our mother entered his vision and made him lose focus of the bigger picture. Javier treats women as pawns for pleasure - nothing more, nothing less. He doesn't respect women at all, not their opinions or thoughts, unless they bore his sons. He liked our mother, but that quickly vanished after she gave birth to two girls. Charlene wasn't content with being pushed to the background, but nothing she did could sway Javier. Once he lost interest, it was over. So she set out to escape.

"Bobby fell into her lap, literally. From the moment he laid eyes on her, he was in love. He asked her to run away with him after they had sex the very first time." An eye roll and a look of disgust before continuing. "She had him so convinced that she and her daughters were in danger and needed to get out that he was willing to throw years of business down the drain to be her savior, but he actually became her destroyer. Charlene was never in any real danger, but in Javier's world she was irrelevant, a piece of pussy to be used at his whim, and that was akin to death for her. With Bobby, she could reinvent herself, and that's exactly what she did. She became Charlene Lloyd and you became Shinah Lloyd." "What happened to you?" Shinah asked quietly.

Royalty was quiet for a long second before answering. "I survived," she said fiercely. "Javier never knew what happened and didn't really care other than the fact that he felt a woman got over on him. Bobby and our father continued to do business and everything was good until it wasn't. Bobby kept his cards close to his vest and never revealed his betrayal, but you are seen by people who were loyal to none but their own self-interest. They paid Javier a visit and tried to leverage that information into a seat at the table, but they read the situation wrong and ended up in shallow graves for their troubles. Javier pretended not to care, but he couldn't figure out the deceit Bobby showed by smiling in his face while harboring his property."

"Property he didn't give a damn about," Bobby interrupted with a snarl.

Royalty glared at him, but did not reprimand him for his interruptions. She continued her story. "The Council of Kings is a global organization made up of every country in the world. A discreet organization who lived and died by its tenets. To be a member of this organization, you had to be invited, or you gained your membership in blood. Once in, there was no out. You were blood bound to honor the Council and its tenets until death, natural or otherwise. Bobby and Javier are both members of this organization, where the identity of its members was such a secret that even knowledge of them could get you buried where you would never be found. There's ten alpha Kings: North America- Canada, and the United States, Western Europe, Japan, the developed market economies, Eastern Europe, Latin America, North Africa, and The Middle East, mainland Africa, South and Southeast Asia, and centrally-planned Asia. These men are like gods to mere mortals. They are beyond powerful and untouchable. They are the top of the food chain, but as we all know, the flow of money goes upwards.

"There are numerous Kingdoms who have permission to operate as long as the tenets of the Council are strictly followed and you can meet your monthly tribute to the Alphas. These men are Kings in their own right, but not as powerful as the Alphas. For instance, the Alpha of North America has broken Canada and the

United States down into sections, mini kingdoms if you will, giving men like Bobby his own territory to run, which for the last twentyfive years has been the east coast from Maine to Florida. Javier's kingdom is Mexico. Despite the affront Bobby had shown him, Javier couldn't just murder another member of the Council without permission. There were protocols to follow and death to any who color outside the lines. So he filed his grievance and was granted leave to handle the problem as he saw fit. Javier had a sick, twisted sense of humor, and he thought it would be poetic justice to send me to deal with the situation."

"Excuse me, but you just said that Javier didn't find any use for females." King was paying attention because he felt that he was about to be thrown into the mix and he didn't want to get caught slipping because he wasn't in the know. "So why would he send you, a female, to handle Council business?" he asked curiously.

Royalty grimaced at the interruption, but decided to indulge her nephew. "Javier had eight sons, each one more sadistic than he was, but he doted on them to the point where they thought they could do anything they wanted to and in his kingdom, they could. I was the only daughter that lived on the compound and it cost me dearly in more ways than one. But I didn't look at my womanhood as a disadvantage like they did, and I showed Javier that I was built to last," she answered cryptically.

"You still didn't answer my question though." King felt like she was trying to spare them and it was too late in the game for that. "Why would he send you?" he asked again.

"Because I murdered every one of his sons until he recognized that I was just, if not more, capable than any dick walking this earth," she said simply as if she just said she had a salad for lunch. When she saw that no further questions were forthcoming, she continued. "Charlene recognized me as soon as she answered her door. We hadn't seen or talked to each other since she left so I didn't expect her to remember the daughter she left behind, but with tears in her eyes, she told me that she could never forget her firstborn. She soon realized why I was there and convinced Javier there were four better ways. She told him that she would get Bobby killed and would hand him the East Coast pipeline on a platter as long as she could run it. The flaw in her plan was that none of the kings words allowed her, a woman, to keep their seat at the table long enough to enjoy it. Javier couldn't back her because it was out of his jurisdiction. So Charlene found a puppet to act as her stand in as she pulled his strings from the shadows." She smirked at Sincere, who grimaced at being called a puppet. "He had to be ambitious and blinded by his greed. Sincere was both and he was to murder Bobby to earn his seat at the table, but as we all know, he turned out to be more resourceful than Charlene imagined. Now she's dead and Bobby's still among the living. A fact that will be remedied very soon," she said seriously.

Everyone looked at Bobby when she made that last statement, but he showed no emotion at his impending death.

Sincere was reeling. He couldn't believe that the man he had come to look at like a father figure was being so passive about this like he had no options but to accept death. Despite everything she had just told them, he saw one unarmed woman talking big talk, and he, for one, wasn't going for it. "Bobby, why are you just standing there like a sheep being led to the slaughter?" he questioned angrily.

Bobby looked at Sincere and smiled sadly. He had come to love him like a son over the years, but he knew eventually that his sins would catch up with him and to be honest, he was tired of running. "Don't worry, son. Everything will be alright. You still have cards to play, but she's right. I've broken the tenets, and better men have been put down for less. The Council is what she says it is: a gift and a curse. But it won't be denied. I owe, and my markers have been called." He turned to Shinah, who still refused to look at him. "Princess, I know you're upset with me, but I did what I did for love. I raised you as my own and never denied you anything, especially my love. I understand what me and your mother's lies cost you and I'm sorry, but I need your forgiveness before I leave this earth," he pleaded softly.

Shinah finally looked at him, but couldn't bring herself to open her mouth to forgive him. His lies cost her too much, so she remained silent.

Bobby sighed when he saw the look in her eyes. He knew he hurt her badly and didn't deserve her forgiveness, He squared his shoulders and faced Royalty, who was staring at him with an amused look on her face. Royalty smirked, but didn't divert the attention from him as she told Shinah to take her young ones to the master bedroom.

"Moosa, take your sister to one of the bedrooms and close the door. Do not come out until I come get you." Shinah didn't plan on leaving with them. Moosa knew better than to argue. He grabbed his sister's hand, who had been uncharacteristically quiet, and walked to one of the bedrooms. He purposely chose one that took them past the bar, where he grabbed a gun before closing the bedroom door behind them. He had learned that it was easier to ask for forgiveness instead of permission.

"Shinah, you don't have to be in here for this," Royalty said, showing uncharacteristic compassion.

"If I'm woman enough to condemn him with my silence, then I'm going to be woman enough to watch him die." Shinah locked eyes with the man who raised her and tried to convert everything she was feeling with that look, hoping it was enough because that was all she could give.

Bobby nodded and smiled at her. It was enough for him. Without another word, he pushed Royalty, trying to close the distance between them. He needed to get his hands on her to have a chance - a slim chance, but a chance nonetheless. Just when he thought he might make it, his momentum was stopped.

Faster than a blink of an eye Royalty had pulled a silenced .22 millimeter pistol from somewhere on her body and shot him in the face. Bobby took another step before stumbling to his knees. He blanched there for a second, staring at nothing before falling on his face with a hole in between his eyes.

Czar looked at King, who shook his head. He hadn't seen where she pulled the pistol from either.

Shinah couldn't make her eyes off of the man who had shown her so much love growing up. She found herself pitying him because he died for a love that was unrequited. She looked up to find her sister staring at her with a look of what? Pity, sympathy… either one annoyed her and she frowned. "What now?" she asked seriously.

Royalty continued to study her for a few seconds before answering. "We earn our seats at the table." She turned to her nephew, who were all eyeing her with a little more respect than before. Murder had a tendency to do that. "Czar, you had a nice little operation going until you got sloppy. Martinez was a King, but as we both know, he's no longer with us.

Raul will take his place. Remove him from the board."

"Raul won't be a problem once he knows the truth about what's what," Czar said seriously. Raul paved the way for him and he wouldn't repay loyalty with anything but.

"Charlene got you that plug, not Raul," Royalty said, reading his mind. "Once he finds out you're the grandson of the woman who murdered his father, he will take you off the boar or risk a frenzy for his territory by the sharks. You have the upper hand, so use it or don't," she added like it didn't matter to her one way or the other. And truthfully, it didn't. She gave him the keys. If he didn't use them and got himself killed, she wouldn't cry over spilled milk. She would just buy another gallon. Czar was still reeling from the fact that Charlene had murdered Martinez.

"Majestic, you have the team to do what you need to do in Jamaica. The Rude Boys are fierce, but unorganized. Get that under control and go get your island back. Terror's ticket has been punched and I'm giving you the green light." Royalty narrowed her eyes angrily when she saw the look of distaste on his face from being given orders by a woman. "You're assuming you have a choice," she said seriously. "Everything hinges on you four controlling your own kingdoms, or everything goes up in flames. You think the Council is only eating from Carter's illegal business?" she asked incredulously. "You can't have one without the other. If you don't do your part, then you brothers fail and the Council will press the button. Let me know if you're in or out because once I walk out that door, the Council will take my report and do whatever will keep their pockets fat." She eyed him until he acquiesced. "I'm in," he told her with a glare. He wouldn't leave his brothers stuck no matter how much he detested drugs.

Royalty nodded and turned to Sincere, who was eyeing him with undisguised hatred. She smirked because she knew that he wouldn't do anything about it. His hands were tied. She almost admired him because he had done well for himself, despite being a puppet. But his time was past and it was then that he knew that. "Sincere, you're officially retired. Hand over the operation to King and enjoy whatever time you have left."

"Retired?" he repeated. He didn't like the taste of the word in his mouth.

"Effective immediately," she said firmly. "On whose authority?" Sincere asked even though he knew it was a stupid question.

Royalty arched an eyebrow to let him know it definitely was a stupid question, but she indulged him anyway. "Mine. The Council doesn't matter because we both know it's going to happen," she said coldly. "Look at this as a way for you and my sister to make up for lost time," she added to give him a way to save face.

Sincere kept his peace because he could read the tea leaves. He had a nice run and wouldn't mind catching up with Shinah. He looked at her and hoped she felt the same way.

"King, your little prison enterprise is genius and something we need to look at expanding in all of our territories." Royalty had been impressed when she was informed of the movies he was making in the prison system; she could imagine the profits once they put it across the country.

King was shocked that she even knew about his activities up north, but he kept his face expressionless and nodded. He realized that he was now playing with the big dogs.

"Make no mistake about what's going on," Royalty said seriously, eyeing everyone in the room. "There are eyes on you, and as soon as they smell blood in the water, they will not hesitate to come for you. My reputation will only stay their hands for so long. So you make your own legends and do it fast, because nothing gets in the way of the Council. You're either a part of the machine or you get chewed up. Charlene put this plan together decades ago, but she didn't get to see it to fruition because she overlooked one important thing." She passed to let it sink in. She needed them to understand that history would not repeat itself. "Even though the queen is powerful, she's still dependent on the king for her protection because if he's not in positions to do so, she can still be set up, captured, and killed. We'll be in touch." She walked towards the elevator. "Someone will be by to retrieve Bobby's body. Some people need to see for themselves that he's actually dead this time." She smirked at Sincere before stepping into the elevator. "Wait!"

Everyone turned to see Moosa standing there with a gun in his hand and his chest poked out. "What about me?" he asked Royalty before the elevator doors could close.

Royalty looked at Shinah, who was frowning at her youngest son, with a smirk before turning to Moosa. "Trust me, you will definitely be a player in this thing of ours. Probably the youngest king on the board." She laughed before letting the elevator close.

Moosa beamed and went back to the bedroom with his sister. He was so happy that it never occurred to him that in order for him to be king, his father would have to be removed from the board.

## CHAPTER 11

Before anyone could say or do anything, the elevator started moving again. The tension was palpable as everyone waited to see who or what would step out. At this point, they were all ready to swear off elevators forever. They all released a collective sigh of relief when a man and woman, both dressed as paramedics, sped off of the elevator pushing a stretcher. They watched as they efficiently loaded Bobby's body onto the stretcher and fixed him up so no one would notice the hole in the middle of his head.

Shinah watched them work with an expression on her face that was hard to decipher. She didn't know how she felt about Bobby's death. On one hand, he loved her, cared for her, and supported her for her whole life, but on the other hand, he betrayed her along with her mother, causing her to leave her children, and that was a sin she couldn't forgive. She glanced over at Sincere when he came to stand beside her. It surprised him to see the grief on his face.

"He really did love you," he said quietly after they disappeared onto the elevator with his body.

Shinah frowned as she thought about what he just said. "I know, he did but some things you just can't come back from," she replied truthfully

Sincere couldn't deny that he wondered if she felt the same way about him. Shinah was about to say something when she was interrupted.

"We don't mean to break up y'all little Love Jones moment, but we need to discuss what just happened," Czar said with a smirk.

Sincere laughed and Shinah rolled her eyes with a smile before saying, "Boy what you know about Love Jones?"

"Believe me, Ma, I know a lot about Love Jones," he replied with a laugh. He grew quiet when he noticed everyone staring at him. "What?" he questioned with a frown.

"You called me Ma," Shinah whispered as she grew emotional.

Czar replayed what he had said in his head and realized that he indeed called her "Ma". He glanced at his brothers and saw that they were staring at him like he was going to explode or something. He shrugged his shoulders and said "Yeah, it's no big deal, ya heard me." He looked at his mother and hit her with his patented smirk.

"I always knew that you would be the one who turned soft first," Shinah said sarcastically with a smile.

Everyone laughed when Czar grimaced.

Shinah father grew exponentially with love as she watched her sons joke with each other. She knew that she would do anything to make sure she never hurt them again. She looked over at Sincere and saw that he was already watching her with an expression of love that left no question about how he felt. She grabbed his hand and squeezed it tenderly. They would have their home, she thought excitedly. "Excuse me, Mommy."

Shinah looked over, saw her daughter standing in the doorway to the bedroom staring at her with her brother behind her shooting daggers her way, and dropped Sincere's hand like it was on fine. She didn't want to show affection to another man in front of them until she talked to them about her and their father. "Yes, baby?"

"Can I meet my brothers now?" Gifted asked seriously. She was unaware of anything that had happened around her, but she knew that the adults would deal with it. She just wanted to meet her brothers.

"Of course you can, pretty lady," King said, taking the reins from their mother. He walked over to his little sister and stuck his hand out. "My name is——" "King, and you're Majestic, Pharaoh, and Czar," she burst out excitedly as he pointed each of them out. "I'm your little sister Gifted," she said happily as she formally introduced herself.

Everyone stared at her with surprise etched onto their features. "How could you tell us apart?" Pharaoh asked, impressed with her intelligence. "How old are you?" "I can tell you apart because you all sound different and you do things differently if you watch closely enough," she explained, sounding a lot older than she was. "Oh, and I'm ten years old," she told them proudly.

"Well nice to meet ye, sistah," Majestic greeted her before he scooped her into his arms.

Gifted squealed in glee as she was lifted into the air. She was beyond happy surrounded by her newfound brothers.

Shinah was overwhelmed with emotion as she watched the scene in front of her. Never in her wildest dreams did she imagine this happening like this. She looked over at Moosa and realized that everything was going so well, but she watched him frown at his little sister so happy with brothers that weren't him. She started to go to him before Sincere grabbed her arm, stopping her. She looked at him confusedly.

"Let me go talk to him, because he's got a lot to get used to," he said sincerely.

Shinah looked at him dubiously, but nodded her assent, grateful that she didn't have to do everything by herself anymore.

Sincere gave her a reassuring smile before making his way over to where Moosa was standing with a scowl on his face. "You know that you will always be her big brother, right?" he told the young boy. Moosa frowned at him, but kept his peace because he knew that he was right. It still didn't make it hurt any less.

"Your mother has had a hard life, but she is the strongest woman I know," Sincere said seriously. "She would never put you and your sister in a bad way. Those are her sons, same as you, but she missed out on their whole lives. As you so eloquently put it, she's been your mother your whole life.

She just met them yesterday," he added mockingly.

Moosa had the decency to look embarrassed. He looked at his brothers and wondered if they would get along, but he put that out of his mind as he turned and looked Sincere in his eyes. "I hear you, old man, but I need you to hear me," he said seriously. "I don't play bout my mother. If you're going to be in her life, then you better take care of her and my brothers and me getting along will be the least of your worries." He maintained eye contact to convey the seriousness of his message.

Sincere wanted to laugh at this young boy threatening him, but he didn't because he understood where he was coming from. He glanced over at Shinah, who was watching them nervously, and vowed to make things right. He looked back at Moosa, who was still grilling him, and smirked. "I got you, young'un. Your mother will always be my top priority," he said seriously.

Moosa nodded, satisfied with his answer. "Well let me go play nice to ease my mom's mind," he grumbled before making his way over to where his sister and brothers were still getting to know each other.

Sincere made his way back over to Shinah. "What happened?" she asked anxiously, never taking her eyes off of her kids.

"Everything will be fine, Shinah," he reassured her. "The question now is, what's next?"

Shinah looked at him and wondered what she did to ever deserve his love. She knew that she wouldn't ever hit him again, even if it killed her. She thought about his question and felt her heart turn cold. She locked eyes with him so he could see the seriousness in hers when she said. "We secure our family's future."

Sincere saw the look in her eyes and knew her innocence was forever gone.. In its place was something hard, something implacable, something that broke his heart because it felt like death.

## CHAPTER 12

Royalty entered the Four Seasons lobby and saw Moses nursing a drink at the bar. She made her way over and took the stool next to him. "Go home, Moses," she told him seriously.

Moses looked over and frowned. When she sat there impassively staring at him like he was nothing, he grew incensed, but he immediately calmed himself when he remembered who he was dealing with. He grimaced because his hands were tied - for the time being, at least. "What about my family?" he asked quietly.

Royalty looked at him incredulously. "You know just as well as I do that you and Shinah are finished," she told him. "You knew the moment she found out Sincere never killed Bobby that you were done." She added salt to the wound.

Moses growled because he knew she spoke the truth, but that didn't make it sting any less. "And my children?" he asked seriously. "I'm sure a visitation will be set up," she said calmly. "I'm sure Shinah wouldn't deny you, seeing that you won't be having any more kids," she added snidely.

Moses glared at her and vowed to see her dead for insolence.

Royalty smirked at him before growing serious. "Stay out of my way, Moses. Don't poke your nose into my business. Stay in your lane. Go home and try to appease your father and you might just make it to old age. Violate, and I won't hesitate to put you down." She maintained eye contact for a second before sliding off of the bat stool and giving him her back as she left the hotel.

Moses watched her leave and knew that he couldn't do anything - not at the moment - but he vowed to repay her for the humiliation and disrespect to his honor. He tossed back the rest of his drink and left the hotel. He needed to get back to Africa as soon as possible.

\*\*\*

Shinah was looking at her four older sons in trepidation after they broke their plan to quickly gain control of their territory.

"We have the pipeline and niggas are loyal to the connect," Czar said seriously as h remembered the harsh lessons he learned while dealing with Jimmy Slim's snake ass. "We put a few people in place to oversee operations and we're golden," he added. He had done what he was proposing. If he could do it with Jimmy Slim's bitch ass, then he could definitely accomplish even more with his brothers.

"It won't be that easy," Sincere said seriously. "If you turn the water on free fall, then you will have every Mexican, white, Blood, Crip and folk trying to be the king of the jungle. Don't forget about the Muslims up north. Knowing the politics of a city goes a long way to keeping the bloodshed down and the feds out of your business." He looked each one of his sons in their eyes to convey the seriousness of the dope game they were about to enter into.

"We just keep everyone in their own jungle," King said simply.

"What do you mean?" Sincere asked curiously. "It's just like in prison. People really venture away from what they know," King said. "The white Supremacists dealt with each other. The Mexicans deal with their own kind, the same with the Bloods, Crips, folks, Muslims, and anybody else that wanted to click up. Each group had a leader who ran his jungle. You feed him and let him feed his people. If he's not making sure everybody is eating, then it guarantees that his run will be a short one," he added giving them the blueprint for dealing with politics.

"So we feed every hood and set it in a state?" Czar asked skeptically. Nobody would make money if everybody had work to sell.

"Nah, bro, we find the strongest of each and feed them," King broke down. "It's a trickle down effect. Let the Bloods deal with the other sets in the state, let the white boys deal with their people, so on and so on. We limit our exposure and we move more dope. We get our money every month and we stay out of the way, or we chop the head off and sew in its place until they realize you don't bite the hand that feeds you," he added menacingly.

"We're missing money by not having our own team out there pitching the work for us," Czar said with a frown. He wasn't too keen on letting somebody else eat off of his plate, especially one he built brick by brick.

King frowned because that was unnecessary exposure and risk.

Sincere saw their differences more clearly now. They were all built the same, but for different reasons. King was more of a director now that he had tasted prison, so he would rather play the shadows and collect money. Yeah, he might be missing some profit, but the difference didn't matter much to him because those were crumbs that could get you sent to prison, a place he was trying to avoid. Czar was a front line, action type of dude who loved the chaos of gun clapping, dope dealing, and counting his own money. He already knew how Majestic got down. The exploits of the Rude Boys were becoming legendary at this point. Pharaoh was the scholar who would legitimize the profits easily that would make their money untouchable.

"Y'all are missing the biggest advantage you have," he told them after putting it together in his head.

The four brothers looked at him, confused as to what he was talking about.

"It's four of you," Sincere started out. "You look alike, act alike, but you all think differently because you are influenced differently."

"And?" Czar said for him to continue. He wasn't seeing the picture he was trying to paint.

"Alone you are powerful and can accomplish a lot as we know, but you're pieces to a machine that hasn't been put together yet." He could see that he had their interests piqued. "King likes to play their background and conduct operations from the shadows. Czar likes to be front line with the soldiers. He loves the excitement that comes with hustling. He loves the drama. Majestic is the muscle who will enforce the law and make sure no one violates. Pharaoh has the brains and the means to legitimize your money so the Feds can't touch you. Stop thinking like individuals and start moving as a whole delegate. Trust in your brothers and watch the machine crush anything in this path. Approach every situation as a team and just trust in each other." Sincere was getting excited just talking about it. If he would've had three more just like him, he felt like he could've taken over the whole world.

"That's brilliant," Pharaoh said quietly as he thought about each individual working in synch towards a common goal. He couldn't find a flaw as long as everyone held up their end.

"The best part of it is," Sincere said when he saw that everyone was on board, "that no one has to know it's four of you."

'What do you mean?" King asked, confused about what he was getting at.

"Make people think you're the same man," Sincere said simply.

Czar burst out laughing because he could already see the advantages. "Never let our potential enemies see us together," he said, rubbing his hands together like a mad scientist. "Exactly." Sincere smiled. "Never speak much and people wouldn't be able to tell the difference. Majestic will only pop up on the scene when it's time to make an example, and that doesn't require too much talking. Pharaoh won't be seen or heard by any of your street people. So the only two in contact with the street dealing enough to be recognized will be King and Czar. Create a mystique around you two that will have men questioning their sanity. Make a man fear death more than he fears prison, and your rat problem will be minimal." He sat back with a smile on his face, feeling good about the plan he had come up with. He looked over at Shinah, who rolled her eyes at him, bringing him down a notch "What?" he asked in response to her look. "You act like you just came up with a cure for cancer," she replied with a smirk "You are feeling yourself way too much," she teased.

Everyone laughed at the look on his face. Even Moosa cracked a smile.

"I mean, it is a good plan for someone who's been hustling since the 80s," King replied with a smile. Sincere took their ribbing on the chin because they were family.

"Pharaoh, ye can take some of de profit and spread it around to de politicians," Majestic said when everyone calmed down.

"Good idea," Pharaoh replied, relishing the idea of owning a couple of senators and congressmen. Everyone was looking at Majestic with respect to his idea. He noticed and rubbed his head in embarrassment.

"What made you come up with that?" King asked curiously. He had to remember that with the type of money they were going to be seeing, bribes would be considered campaign contributions or donations. Majestic looked at him for a few seconds to see if he was making fun of him, but when he saw that he really wanted to know, he answered, "Mem bene bred to be a leader of men since me can remember," he said quietly as he remembered the many lessons Buju taught him as he grew up. "Politics, de ins and outs were a part of dat," he added seriously. King nodded and sat back, satisfied with his answer. "With that being said, the main objective is to protect the people in this room," Shinah said seriously as she made eye contact with each of her children. "I'm not the sheltered and naive woman I was over twenty years ago. I'm not without means to provide you assistance if you need it. My sister thinks we're ignorant to the game we've been thrust into, but I've been underestimated many a time in my life, and I want you to take this wherever you go from this point forward. Any violation against this family will be answered in kind, but times ten. Family first, so protect those you love with everything you got," she added with finality.

Everyone was solemn as they digested everything she had said.

Sincere looked at Shinah until he caught her eyes. What he saw in them just confirmed what he already knew. Any vestige of the lost and scared woman who was headed down the rabbit hole twenty plus years ago when they met was no longer residing inside of her. In her place he saw a woman battle hardened by life, scarred, but wearing them proudly as badges of honor. He saw a mother who was willing to do whatever she needed to do to right the wrongs of her past. He saw a woman he wanted to spend the rest of his life with.

## CHAPTER 13

Back in his ride after the meeting finished, Majestic took a deep breath and thought about everything that had transpired in his life over the last twentyfour hours. He went to grab Buju's lion head medallion and grimaced as he remembered snatching it off before tossing it at his sister's feet. He frowned as he envisioned Buju's look of disappointment at how he reacted to the news of his adoption. He smirked as he heard his voice in his head telling him over and over again, "Grab ye nuts, bwoy, to make sure ye still a man because only women let 'erat rude de mind.' He wondered if somehow Buju knew what he would be faced with one day and prepared him as best he could for the difficult decision he would have to make. "Ye going 'ome, brudda?" the driver asked respectfully, breaking his reminiscing mood.

Majestic looked up and caught the eyes staring at him through the rearview mirror. The man was one of the few he trusted to drive him around when he needed to be somewhere. The Rude Boys owned and operated a couple dozen taxi cabs in and around the city. It was one of the ways they stated in the loop with the underworld of Miami. He saw the sincerity and loyalty staring back at him, an eagerness to please him, but wondered if that loyalty could be turned into betrayal for the right price. With a start, he realized that this was what Buju's training was preparing him for: to measure the words of men against their actions. To balance life and death on his word. To be a leader of men. He also realized that Buju did not entrust his legacy to a stranger. He placed it into his hand - a man not of his blood, but no less his son.

He looked at the eyes still watching him with a new awareness and knew that he was prepared for what was to come. "No, be patient wit' mem. Mem wan' to ride around fa a bit to clear mem 'ind."

The driver smiled back as he turned the key to cut the car on. "Don't ye worry, brudda. Just rest easy as mem drive ye around," he said as he pulled into traffic. "Ye safe wit' mem, brudda, mem word on dat," he added seriously.

Majestic nodded and closed his eyes. He leaned his head back and allowed himself a brief respite to plan his next move. If he would've been paying more attention, then he would have noticed that he wasn't the only one out for a leisurely drive.

Czar arrived back at the room to find Dior asleep in their bed. He quickly undressed and slid under the covers with her. The meeting with his family made him confront a lot of issues he had buried deep, but also made him realize how alone he really was before he came into his life. After his adopted mother was sent to prison, he never allowed people to get

too close because it was hard to trust their true intentions, especially after he was all the way up, but now he was placing his life into the hands of his brothers. Although they looked like him, they were not him, and that was a cause for concern because he moved off of street bred instinct that had kept him alive more times than he could remember. But now he was one part to a whole and he could be killed because someone other than himself fucked up. It made him appreciate the constant and familiar this in his life.

He looked down at Dior and knew that she loved him, knew that she should go to the ends of the earth with him, but he didn't know if he could be everything she needed him to be. She knew his deepest secrets and had never hesitated to pick him back up. She had put herself on the back burner and awaited her turn when he was with Chrissy. Plain and simple, the woman put him before herself and anybody else. He wrapped his arms around her and pulled her back into his body. As soon as her soft ass nestled against his dick, she moaned and he hardened. Without hesitation, he lifted her left leg and slid his dick into her.

"Oh my God," Dior moaned when she felt him enter her. "I love you, Czar." She began to push back, fucking him too.

Czar just growled as he flipped her onto her stomach and went to work.

"Oh...my...God! You're so deep, baby!" she screamed as he started digging her out. I...love... you. I...love...you. I love you," she moaned as he slow stroked her into submission Czar pumped himself in and out of her wet pussy as he concentrated on her orgasm before he erupted. When he felt her contracting around his dick, signaling her climax, he couldn't hold it any longer. He didn't know if he could be everything she needed, but he would give her everything he had.

*****

"So we're doing it big like this now, son?" Tango asked in awe as they boarded the private jet.

King smirked at his closest comrade as he watched him admire the cabin of the plane. He couldn't front; the private jet was immaculate. But just because he wasn't used to this level of opulence didn't mean he was overly impressed with it. He wasn't used to moving how he was now  but he would take to it like a duck to water and make sure he dotted all of his i's and crossed all of his t's so the ship wouldn't sink once they set sail.

"I told you, we're playing on a different level now," he joked with Tango. "So get used to all of this because there's no looking back now."

"I feel that, dog. I just got out of prison a few days ago and it feels like I'm stepping into a Godfather movie," Tango said seriously. "The shit we ran into or was pulled into down here let me know we were dealing with a different breed of cat, but if we're going to be playing on this level, then we all in because there's no looking back. It's only death for me, son. I'm never going back to the box," he added with finality.

King was nodding his head in agreement before Tango even finished talking because he was of the same mind. "I'm with you on that, fam, but we gotta make sure all of our ducks are in a row. All of that old tradition shit is out of the window. We're about to make waves because we're going to revolutionize the drug game," he said enthusiastically. "These old heads have gotten fat and lazy. That shit is over. We need young and hungry niggas ready to earn their keep and not rock the boat."

Tango felt a smile blossom on his face as he listened to King. "I know just the niggas we need to get with," he said cryptically.

King looked at him curiously. "Who?"

"These little gang niggas," Tango said seriously. "I know most are wild and seem out of control, but that's because they didn't have a way to eat. If we provide the food, we got a ready-made machine willing to do anything to keep a full belly."

"Son, I was just telling my family the exact same thing," King said. "I took the concept from prison. Everybody already has their own territory and soldiers. We plug them in and reap the rewards," he added simply.

"We're gonna have to make a few examples with these old heads," Tango said seriously. "These niggas not going to just let us push them out." "They will either retire and enjoy the fruits of their labor on a beach somewhere, or they will get retired and fitted for a boc," King said seriously. He knew some niggas wouldn't like the new management, but they would adapt if they wanted to keep working or living.

Tango looked at King and saw some of the vicious young pitbull he met years ago when they hit the yard up north. Niggas had learned the hard way about underestimating the young boy, but he knew better. He had no doubt they would accomplish their goals or go down in history for down the demonstration they were about to put down. Either way, he was down for the ride. "Let's throw a retirement party then, my nigga."

***

Pharaoh was riding in the back of his chauffeured Yukon Denali with the head of his security team, Lion, breaking down his plans for him.

"I've been knowing you since we were boys, Leo," he said, addressing the man by his birth name. "We both know that the streets don't approve of me stepping into my father's shoes, so I'm giving you free reign to bring them to order any way you see fit. You have carte blanche to make sure my family's hold on the streets is unquestioned," he finished dangerously.

Lion nodded, accepting his task without question. "What will you do?" he asked curiously. His voice sounded like a diesel engine getting revved up.

Pharaoh smirked, but instantly turns serious. "Make sure we don't get buried," he answered truthfully "Either in a penitentiary or a grave."

## CHAPTER 14

Shinah was watching Sincere fix them a couple of drinks, not sure what to say or do. For the last few hours after their boys had left, he had taken the time to get to know her two youngest children. It meant a lot to her because it had shown her that the man she had met so long ago had not changed as much as she thought he did. Over the years, she had envisioned him as money hungry, a sadistic monster who had destroyed her life because those thoughts gave her an excuse not to love him. She had created a man in her mind that she wouldn't have a problem killing when the time came. But seeing him now - older, wiser, a little more cynical, but overall still the same man she met twenty-five years ago - had her realizing that she had never stopped loving him. Now they were alone after she sent the kids to bed and she was as nervous now as she was that time she first went to buy crack, meeting him that fateful day. She remembered him wading into the mass of derelict, dirty crackheads standing in line to buy their next high to get to her. She remembered his continuing attempts to help her despite her never asking him for it. She smirked as she remembered how he used to take the scenic route to spend more time with her before selling her what she wanted and she let her smirk bloom into a full smile as she remembered the friendly bribes of trips out to eat, trips to the movies, and to miniature golf to get to know her. She had to admit that she enjoyed those outings despite what she made him believe because those hours with him were a respite from the hell she was building for herself. She remembered him refusing to sell her anything else because he couldn't keep destroying her life. He told her that he was no better than Roland, her ex, who tricked her into smoking in the first place, if he kept contributing to her downfall.

So he cut her off, but told her he would be there if she ever needed him, and he kept his word by taking her in when she had nowhere else to go. She remembered him making love to her and then her betraying him. She remembered the look on his face when he saw her sitting in his dope house about nine months pregnant. She remembered him taking her to the hospital and footing the bill when her parents cut her off. He had never done anything other than try to take care of her and she repaid him with betrayal every time.

"Here."

She snapped out of her reverie when she heard his voice and looked up to see him staring at him as he held her drink out to her. She grabbed the tumbler of liquor from his hand, mumbled her thanks, and averted her eyes because she felt like he could read her thoughts.

"Still running from me, Shinah?"

She turned, ready to curse him out, until he saw that he was teasing her. She blushed when she noticed that same intense look in his eyes, but she forced herself not to turn away that time. He was right. It was time to stop running. "I'm done running, Sincere," she said honestly.

He continued to look at her for a few seconds before nodding his head. "Been a hell of a couple days, huh?" he asked to ease the tension in the room that had suddenly appeared.

Shinah narrowed her eyes at him before he burst into laughter. "That was so corny," she told him between laughs.

Sincere couldn't help but laugh along with her because he realized that he was being corny, but he suddenly grew serious. "I've never stopped loving you."

"Sincere——" she started before he cut her off.

"Whoa, whoa, let me finish please," he said as he stopped whatever she was about to say. "From the moment I saw you standing in my line to buy some work, I knew you didn't belong. I mean, you were driving the same kind of car I was driving, and I was the drug dealer." He chuckled before continuing. "We were as different as day and night, but you were stepping into my world, a world where I knew you didn't belong, and I wanted to help you. It wasn't long before I was in love with you, but you

were in love with something stronger." Shinah lowered her lead in shame.

Sincere reached over, lifted her head and looked into her eyes… "When I found out Charlene was the one contracting me, I knew something wasn't right. I asked her how you were doing and she lied, said you were overseas recovering, when in fact you were in the hospital where I left you. When I went to see Bobby, he was expecting me, waiting for me, actually, and the only reason I'm still alive today is because of my love for you and those babies in your stomach. Even though I didn't know at the time it was four of them in there." He smirked before going on. "He actually thought I was sent by the Council of Kings, but he never expected it to be Charlene who pushed the button. He was having problems with the Council and decided to use Charlene's treachery to his advantage. That's when he came up with the idea of faking his death. No one, especially Charlene, questioned the lack of body because I had his watch, which he gave me, and that was all the evidence she needed of his demise. Before sending me home, Bobby gave me his secrets about the Council, about Charlene, and you but he did it anyway because he genuinely loved your mother. Javier didn't want Charlene. He wanted to own her, and Bobby thought he was saving her form hell. But unbeknownst to him, he was inviting a snake into his bed. I never had a way to contact Bobby, but he would get at me periodically over the yeas and give me instructions. I trusted him with my life and over time I came to love him. He never stopped looking for you. I never stopped. But eventually hope runs out. To be honest, your running away probably saved all of our lives: - mine, yours, and your sons - because we didn't know how serious the game we were playing was. So I need you to let all of those feelings go because I don't want to waste any more time on the past. We have to make sure our family is still standing when the end game is near, but I need to know that you're in this with me, that you don't forsake me again." He looked at her intently, not realizing that he was holding his breath.

Shinah had tears streaming down her face, but she didn't flinch away as she met his gaze. "I will never forsake you or our children ever again. Now please get over here and kiss me," she said softly. "I thought you would never ask," Sincere said before capturing her lips with his own. He didn't know how much time he had with her, but he would cherish every seconds.

***

Majestic still hadn't gone home. He was sitting in a lounge called Trinity's, which was owned by the sister of one of his brethren, nursing a glass of Hennessy and still trying to make sense of the last twenty-four hours. He sighed and was about to call it a night when he felt her watching. He couldn't tell you how he knew it was the woman from his family's restaurant earlier that day that was watching him. He just knew. He grew excited because he knew that he was being stalked. For what reason, he didn't know, but he was too stoned to believe that it was a coincidence. He caught the eye of the bartender and gave him a prearranged signal before getting up and heading towards the exit. Unless he missed his guess, she would follow shortly.

Chaka couldn't believe her luck when her young Lion walked into Trinity's and sat at the bar. She almost went to him, then but decided against it. She wanted to see if he would notice her. As she sat there watching him, she couldn't help but to admire him. There was nothing more enticing to her than a sexy man who didn't know the effect he had on the opposite sex. She could tell that he had a lot on his shoulders and she could well imagine what it was, especially after seeing the Red Viper at the hotel earlier. She was aware of Royalty Salvatore's reputation because they both ran in the same circles. She knew that she was Javier's enforcer and wouldn't be in the States without cause. Her young Lion seemed to keep dangerous company, but that only excited her more. She couldn't stand a square, boring man. After about twenty minutes, she was about to go to him when she saw him leaving the lounge. She almost forgot her training and ran after him, but she calmed down and waited five minutes before getting up to leave. She tossed a couple of twenties onto the table before casually strolling out of the bar.

"If mem dinna know betta, mem would tink dat ye are following mem," a voice said from the shadows.

A smile formed on Chaka's face as she slowly turned towards the voice. She didn't want to make any sudden moves and accidentally get shot, but she couldn't help feeling confident when she said, "Andi mem twas, den wat?"

Majestic was taken aback by the casualness of her words because the challenge was clear in her voice. He knew that the shooters were in position, so he stepped out of the shadow to allow himself to be seen. "Den mem would have a problem dat needs fixin'," he said in a tone that didn't leave one guessing his intentions.

Chaka's smile grew as she watched her young Lion step out of the shadows, clutching a gun in his right hand. She couldn't believe how turned on she was at that moment. "Tell ye men ta stand down. Mem 'armless," she said, letting him know that she was more than he was seeing.

Majestic was shocked that she knew about his men, but he didn't let it show on his face. Her revealing knowledge about these shooters let him know not to take her lightly, but he couldn't deny that he was intrigued. He studied her and had to admit that she was beautiful, but there was an animal magnetism about her that called to him. "Me doubt dat ye are 'armless" he said seriously. "Wat do ye want wit' mem?" he asked curiously.

Chaka thought about playing with him some more, but decided to end the games. "Fa ye ta fuck mem," she said bluntly.

Majestic chuckled because he knew that he had never met a woman like her before. He wasn't one to think with his lower self, but he needed to release some of the stress he had been carrying around for a while now, He wasn't sure that she didn't mean him any harm, but at the moment, he was ready to find out. He didn't know where this sudden urge to be reckless came from, but it felt good. "Unless ye into public sex, lead de way," he challenged her.

"Slow down, young Lion," she said as she led the way to her car. "Dis only de first date. We'll do it in pubic in de morning," she added with a laugh, Majestic shook his head as he slid into the passenger seat. The woman was pleasure and pain and he was sure that the world cause him a lot of both before it was all said and done.

*** 

King and Tango disembarked from the place after landing at Teterboro Airport in New Jersey to find two town cars waiting to take them wherever they needed to go.

"I could really get used to this boss shit!" Tango exclaimed after stretching and watching their luggage being loaded into the cars.

"Well, get used to it, dog, because there's no looking back," King said sincerely.

Tango looked at him and grew serious for a second. "Real shit, fam, I want to say thank you because not too many niggas get out here and remember the men they bidded with. You kept your word and went above and beyond for me. You have my loyalty," he said seriously

King appreciated the love, but he didn't need it because men kept their word and boys spoke words. "What's overstated doesn't need to be explained, fam," he said as he dapped his comrade up. Tango nodded and let his smile bloom back onto his face. He had a mischievous glint in his eyes as he looked at the king. "You betta get home before wifey put dat ass on house arrest," he said, laughing.

King laughed along with him and dapped him up again before sliding into his town car. He was about to send Latoya a text letting her know that he was onto what had happened and knew that her mind was going to be blown once he told her all of it. He had big plans for her now that he was set up to do as he pleased. He just hoped she was ready for it, because there wouldn't be time for second guessing once he pressed the button on the rise to the top. About forty-five minutes later, the town car slid to a stop in front of his brownstone. He grabbed his bag, tipped the driver, and bounded up the steps. He stuck his key in the lock and pushed open the door as quietly as possible. He seat his bag down in the foyer and went to find his lady. He searched her office, but found it empty, so he made his way to their bedroom to find her asleep in their bed surrounded by paperwork from one of her cases and her laptop.

He walked over and softly kissed her on the lips. "Ummmm," she moaned as she slowly opened her eyes. "Hey baby, when did you get in?" she asked as she nibbled on his lips, kissing him back.

Just now. But I need you to come take a shower with me," he whispered as she started getting undressed. Now that he was in her presence, he couldn't wait to fill her up.

Latoya felt her pussy thump as she watched him shed his clothes. When he was completely nude and she saw that he was sharp and ready for her, she almost came from that visual alone. "Someone sure did miss me," She teased as he scooped her into his arms. "You better put me back to sleep too, mister," she added in anticipation of what was to come.

King looked at her to let her see the hunger in his eyes for her. He was about to make her pay for that comment. "When have I ever not made you tap out?" he asked with a smile as he carried her to the bathroom.

"Promise, promises," she taunted in his ear before sucking on his earlobe. She couldn't wait to show him that he wasn't the only one missing somebody.

## CHAPTER 15

Dior awoke to find the bed she shared with Czar empty. She stretched and groaned when she felt the soreness in her body. She didn't mind it because it was the good kind of soreness, the kind of soreness that let you know that your man had put in the work. She was about to go back to sleep when she heard knocking at the door. As bad as she wanted to ignore it, she knew that it could be important and she didn't want to hear Czar's mouth if she made him miss something because she was being lazy. So she got up and threw on a robe before making her way to the door. "Who is it?" she asked impatiently. "Bitch, open the door," Bianca answered from the other side.

Dior hurriedly unlocked the door and ran to it to let her best friend in.

Bianca was about to go in on her for taking so long to answer the door until she saw the look on her face - the look that said she had some good dick last night. "Bitch, I hate yo," she growled playfully before pushing her way past her into her room. "What?" Dior asked innocently as she couldn't seem to be able to stop smiling.

"What!" Bianca mimicked perfectly. "That silly-ass grin on your face lets me know you got some dick last night and I'm jealous," she added with a playful pout.

"Bitch, I don't know what was on his mind last night, but when he came in, he woke me up by sliding up in me from the spoon position. Oh my God, it was soooo good." She shivered just thinking about it. "We were making love and we didn't use protection at all," she added, wondering if that meant that he was ready to take their relationship to the next level - the until death do them part level. "Well, I'm happy for you girl," Bianca said genuinely. "Lord knows you've been waiting on it forever. I, for one, am glad that I won't have to hear you bitching and moaning about him doing you dirty," she added playfully.

"Whatever, hoe," Dior said with a laugh. "What are we getting into today?" she asked curiously as she picked up the phone to order some breakfast from room service

Bianca just held up two sets of car keys. The smile on her face showed all of her teeth.

"What are those?" Dior asked as she watched her friend damn near levitate with excitement. "The keys to two BMW drop top coupes," she said excitedly.

"Whose are those?" Dior asked with a smile at her friend's happiness.

Bianca looked at her like she was crazy. "Ours, bitch."

Now Dior looked confused. "How did we get two BMW's?" she asked suspiciously. "Czar just gave us two cars?" Dior asked, confused. She knew that her man was generous, but two cars was a bit much. "Yeah, his brothers was flying back to New York last night and didn't want to have the cars shipped, so he just gave them to Czar, who gifted them to us," Bianca said, imagining herself stunting on the haters. "So which one do you want?" she asked, holding up a set of keys in each hand. "The green one or the grey one?"

"You know money make the pussy go whoo, whoo," Dior joked before grabbing the keys to the green one "Where is Czar?" she asked.

"He said he had to holla at his brother before we left," Bianca said as she debated with herself whether to paint her car bubble gum pink or Dallas Cowboy blue.

"Well, let's get ready to go shopping and stunt on these Florida bitches before we get back to NOLA," Dior said excitedly.

"You already know we are about to make these hoes mad," Bianca said, twerking a little bit.

They both burst out laughing as they went to get ready to shine on Miami Beach.

*** 

King and Latoya were eating breakfast as he told her the events of the last forty-eight hours. "You're telling me you have three identical brothers?" she asked in disbelief. She was enthralled as she listened to his story. It sounded like a movie to her.

"Yeah, love, there are three more of me in this world," he replied with a smirk.

Latoya groaned as she thought about dealing with four Kings instead of one.

King laughed at her. "You act like this the worst thing on the earth.

Latoya rolled her eyes at him. "Are they as arrogant as you are, pompous ass?" she asked with a smirk. "We wouldn't be identical if they weren't, ma," he replied with a smirk of his own.

"So when do I get to meet them?" she asked curiously. Now that her interest was piqued, she had to meet them for herself. "Soon," he said simply

Latoya narrowed their eyes as she looked at him because she knew that he was keeping something from her.

"What?" he asked when he noticed her look. He knew that she was on to him, but he would make her work for it. Her tenacity was one of the traits that made her a great lawyer. "Don't 'what' me, King," she said slowly, letting him know that she was on his trail. "What aren't you telling me?" she asked sternly.

King decided not to drag it out any longer because he wanted her to know. It was one of the main reasons he left Miami earlier than he planned to. He got up, left the room, and retrieved the folder his brother Pharaoh had given him and his brothers. Once he was back in the kitchen, he slid it over to her without a word.

Latoya slid the contents out of the folder and quickly perused the paperwork in front of her. She looked up at him in disbelief. "Is this for real?" she asked in shock.

"Yes, it's legit, ma," King said, amused at her reaction. "My brother Pharaoh gifted me and our other two brothers that the day we met him," he told her truthfully.

Latoya got up and ran out of the kitchen. Before King could ask her what she had done, she walked back in carrying her laptop. After typing for a few minutes, she looked up at King. "Your brother gave you stock in one of the biggest pharmaceutical companies in the country. Tri-med traded on the stock exchange. He gave you roughly fifty million in stock in that company. About another thirty million in assets, and he gave you twenty million cash in a bank account." She couldn't believe a brother he had never met before had blessed him like this. This was generational wealth, to say the least.

King had already had time to digest the numbers, so they weren't having the same effect anymore. Plus he knew that if everything went according to plan, then he would get those same numbers on his own. He pulled a velvet ring box out of his pocket and set it in her line of sight while she was doing more research on her laptop. He had bought the ring while in Miami after meeting his family because they were about to put everything on the line with this move they were about to undertake. He also wanted to secure her because he realized that she had been down for him from the beginning and he knew her love for him was pure.

"Latoya." He knew that calling her name would get her attention. When she looked up at him, he used eyes to put her attention on the ring box.

"What's this?" she asked, picking it up. When she opened it, her eyes grew wide and she screamed. "Nigga, don't fucking play wit' me." All of her professionalism went out of the window as she stared at the five carat princess cut diamond in a rose gold band.

"T, you've shown me nothing but love and loyalty from the day we met. You've always had my best interest at heart, even when I was too stubborn to see it. I love you, and if I'm being real, I have for a very long time. Will you be my number one until we're both dust scattered to the wind?" He wasn't being conventional, but he was sincere.

Latoya sat there staring at him with tears running down her face. For so long she had dreamed of becoming his wife, and now it was happening. It was surreal.

"You want me to get down on one knee?" he joked when she hadn't answered him. He wasn't feeling getting on his knees, but he would do it to appease her.

Latoya got up and made her way over to him. She hugged him as she continued crying. "I always respected your intelligence, King, but I started to doubt that this would ever happen. You've showed me that you're truly a king in more than name, and I would like to be your forever queen," she whispered into his ear. "And for your information, the only time I want you on your knees is when you're making love to me from behind," she teased. "Now put my ring on," she ordered him playfully as she handed him the velvet box.

King did just that before tossing her over his shoulder and taking her to get in position while he got on his knees.

\*\*\*

Chaka watched her young Lion as he got dressed and wondered why she was so attracted to him. She had met richer men, she had sexed more powerful men, she had been attracted to some of her targets before, she had even loved a few men, but none made her feel like her young Lion. It was like he possessed this magnetism that had her stuck in its pull. He was electrifying and didn't seem to realize it. His potential was alluring and if she didn't watch herself, she would find herself following his lead instead of the other way around.

"Can mem see ye again?" she asked demurely. She didn't want to show him her true self just yet and run him away.

Majestic glanced her way and saw her watching him get dressed like a rattlesnake about to enjoy dinner. The look was somewhat discomforting to him, but it also turned him on. Last night they didn't waste time on words because the sex didn't call for it.

They commanded each other with grunts, moans, and sighs, and somehow it was enough. He knew that she was more than she was revealing, but so was he.

"Mem will see ye again when mem finishes mem business," he said seriously. He didn't even know if he had time to entertain a woman in his life with everything he had going on, but even as that thought crossed his mind, he knew that he would make time for her. "Mem will see ye ta night if mem can," he added with a grimace as he saw the frown on her face.

Chaka smiled brightly as he agreed to see her again that night. She couldn't explain her hunger for him, but now that she had her fill, she wouldn't stop until she was full.

\*\*\*

When Dior and Bianca returned to the room after going shopping, they found Czar there waiting on them.

"Y'all sure enough money was spent?" he asked sarcastically when he saw all of the shopping bags.

"Boy, it ain't like we spent your money," Dior joked as she dropped her bags and ran over to hug him. It was the first time she had seen him all day and she missed him. Bianca just rolled her eyes at them.

Czar looked down at Dior hugging on him and couldn't help the smile that blossomed into his face. He had a different outlook on life since he had met his family, and it had him looking at the bigger picture. Dior was definitely going to be a part of that picture.

"Are you sure you're not one of Czar's brothers?" Bianca asked dubiously when she saw the look on his face as he looked at Dior.

Dior looked confused at her question, but Czar grasped what she was gettin at instantly and laughed.

"Nah, B, it's me," he said, chuckling. "We're playing on a different level now and I have to make sure the people in my life that I trust the most are taken care of, starting with you two," he added seriously.

"Awwwww," they both said at the same time. Czar frowned at them both before continuing. "Seriously though, y'all both held me down when niggas were turning on me and I appreciate the loyalty. Y'all are my family and as long as you kept it solid with me, then I'll always do the same."

"We got you, daddy," Dior said, hugging him tighter.

"You already know we're team Czar," Bianca told him sincerely.

"Well, let's get back to N'awlins," he said seriously.

"I have some people to see."

***

Majestic walked into his family's restaurant to find it strangely empty. Usually it would be teeming with people enjoying breakfast, but it was eerily quiet, and that made him draw his pistol. He looked around for a sign of what was going on, but he saw no one, not even Mega, and he heard not a sound. His mind instantly went to his sisters and he hoped they were all right. He started to feel guilty about spending the night with a woman he barely knew when his family might've been in trouble. He put that out of his mind to focus on the task at hand: making sure his sisters were okay. He made his way towards the office to see if they were there. He wanted to call out, but something told him not to. As he got closer, he started to relax because he heard his sisters' voices, but his guard instantly went back up when he heard men's voices also. His anger rose as he thought his sisters were shutting the restaurant down and missing money to spend time with some men. No longer worried about stealth, he stepped into the room to find his sisters entertaining three men in suits. He instantly recognized that they were Jamaican and he recognized the self-assurance of men who were powerful and comfortable with that power. Of course all conversation had stopped and all eyes were on him, but he was content to let the silence build because he wasn't a guest. He was at home, and if a man paid a visit to your house, then he had better announce himself before something happened to him. "Brudda…"

Majestic cut his eyes at her and she immediately shut up.

One of the men saw this and chuckled. He looked at Majestic as if appraising the man. After a few seconds, he nodded as if he liked what he saw. "Majestic Livingston, the only male heir to Buju and Sasha Livingston. Protector, provider and planner for Star and Sky Livingston. Leader of the infamous Rude Bwoys." The man let it be known that he was well versed in who he was. "I'm here on behalf of the people of Jamaica. My name——"

"Nicholas."

Nicholas let a smile grow into his face when his name was spoken. His estimation of the young man grew a little more. "So Buju did tell you about me," he said seriously. "I was starting to wonder," he added snidely.

"What are ye doing 'ere?" Majestic asked quietly.

"Terror is dead," Nicholas bluntly stated.

Majestic kept a straight face because he didn't want it known how much that news affected him. He didn't care that Terror was dead; only hat he wasn't the one who sent him on his way. "And?". Nicholas smirked at the coolness of his response. If Majestic was as vicious as the reports he had read said, he respected his self-control. He, for one, knew firsthand how the thirst for revenge can cause you to lose all you hold dear. "I was your father's most trusted lieutenant and would gladly give my life for him or Sasha."

"Den where were ye when dey both died?" Majestic asked, interrupting him with no regard for his rudeness. Hearing how he give his life for Buju and Sasha made him angry because it only exacerbated the fact that he couldn't stop either one from slinging their lives, even though one was unavoidable. Nicholas acknowledged his right to be angry, but didn't react to it in a visible way. The next words out of his mouth were calm, but laced with steel. "Your father had a dream that was bigger than any of us could see, but we didn't doubt him for one moment. When he sent me away to the U.K. for school I hated leaving, but I did it because I believed in Buju. Every man in this room would have gladly given his life for your father, and there are hundreds more who will know the same for you. My Young Lion, I speak for those men now as I pledge our loyalty and love to you and your family. Will you accept your rightful place at the head of our table?"

Majestic looked at his two sisters and saw that they were staring at him with trepidation. He knew that they wondered if he would say anything about the adoption, but he wouldn't, because that wasn't their business. He felt fraudulent because he knew that he wasn't their real son and entitled to nothing, but he also felt an obligation to Buju to do what he said he was going to do: keep the Lion alive. He was torn and didn't know what to do.

Nicholas saw the indecision warring inside of him and stood up. He walked over to Majestic and placed a comforting hand upon his shoulder. "Buju gave me a message to give to you, but didn't tell me when to share this with you. He said that I would know what to do when the weight of the world seemed to be on your shoulders. That message didn't make much sense to me until this very moment." He marveled at his dearest friend's ability to navigate the great unknown called the future. "He said to tell you that you are his son, not by blood, but by deed. Blood can be corrupted, but loyalty can never be bought or taken away if truly given. He said that they prepared you to be great and now you're standing on the precipice of that greatness. Livingston's don't shirk their responsibilities. They do what must be done despite the pain or consequences. Do you not think I loved my Sasha and my two daughters, your sisters, because I sent them away? I did it to remove my greatest weakness beyond our enemies reach. I kept you by my side because I needed to prepare you for what was to come. I will die in peace because I know, without a doubt, that you will rise to the occasion. As much as I love your mother and sisters, you, my son, are my greatest creation. The lion has always been inside of you."

When he finished, Majestic had tears flowing down his face. He felt his father Buju in those words and it removed any doubt he had about his path. He looked over at his sisters and saw that they both had tears flowing from their eyes. They were looking at him with something akin to awe and it brought home his destiny. He looked back at Nicholas and nodded his assent.

"Now the real work begins," Nicholas said seriously. "There are a few important people in the city who would like to meet you," he added anxiously. Now that the first step was taken, he was ready to see it through.

Majestic nodded, still too overcome with emotion to speak.

"Brudda!" Sky called out before he could leave. Majestic turned around and saw that she was holding their father's lion head necklace out to him with an expectant look on her face. He looked at the medallion and remembered how powerful he felt the moment he put it on. He couldn't lie to himself any longer. He bent his head and let her slide it onto his neck.

"Now ye ready, brudda," she said quietly when she adjusted the necklace to sit right on his chest. He looked at both of his sisters and let his eyes express what he couldn't say at that moment. He kissed them each on the cheek before following Nicolas and his men out of the restaurant. He was ready to let his lion roar.

***

Royalty was enjoying a brief respite from her daily grind when her phone rang, shattering her artificial peace. She picked up the device she wished she could do without and frowned at it when she saw her father's numbers flashing across the LED screen. She wanted to ignore him, but knew that if she did, he would keep trying until she answered. So she took a deep breath and decided to get it over with. "Yes, Padre?" She didn't bother to hide her annoyance at his interruption. "Report," he demanded in a gruff voice.

Royalty grimaced when she heard his disrespectful tone. No matter how much she accomplished, he never acknowledged it. Even when she told him that she had killed every one of his sons, he never batted an eye, and no matter how many times she told herself that it didn't matter, it still bothered her. Her therapist would say that deep down inside, she was still a little girl searching for her father's approval - or he would've said it if she didn't kill him after he said it to her the first time.

"Everything is going according to plan. All the players are in position to execute your vision. Charlene is dead, as is Bobby. Sincere didn't balk at his forced retirement and the east coast will be open for business sooner rather than later." She delivered her report in a robotic monotone.

"Do you think that my grandsons are up to the task I set before them?" he asked curiously.

She rolled her eyes because he was always taking credit for some work she had put in. "Despite the enormity of the task I've placed in front of them, they seem more than capable of pulling it off," she said with grudging respect. She had to admit, even if it was just to herself, that her nephews were gorillas in a land full of monkeys. She couldn't wait to unleash them

"And how is your sister?" he asked in a soft tone that confused her.

"She also seems capable," she answered simply. "Good, good," he said cryptically. "When all is to my liking, kill them all," he added before hanging up.

Royalty looked at her phone with a frown after he had hung up. She had known all along what his end games was, but after meeting her family, she wasn't sure if she still felt the same way. One thing for sure, if she went against her father, they better be ready for the war he was sure to bring to their doorstep.

Vincent "Vitto" Holloway

**CHAPTER 16 One Year later...**

Gauge was constantly looking over his shoulder as he made his moves because Czar was back in the city and he wasn't taking any prisoners. If you ever rocked with that snake Jimmy Slim, then he was putting you down, no questions asked. He violated in the worst way when he turned on Czar for a few dollars. What made it even worse was the fact that Czar was the one who put food on his table for him and his family, then made it possible to get them out of the slums. But when Czar showed up at his door looking for an ally, for help, he repaid him with betrayal. When he found out that the team that Jimmy Slim sent missed, he immediately got in the wind. He knew how Czar gave it up. Hell, he had seen him in action more times than he could count. So he had dipped to this little chick's spot in Baton Rouge until he could figure something out. But then Jimmy Slim had gotten himself murdered at a club in Miami. Rumor was that he was killed during a drug deal turned robbery, but he knew better. When he had heard that Jimmy Slim had a closed casket funeral, he knew without a doubt that Czar had put his grave diggers to work once again. He was scared to leave the house at first, but as the months went by, he started slipping in and out of New Orleans to make a couple of plays here and there to keep some money in his pockets. The longer Czar kept him alive, the more emboldened he became to the point where he wasn't even trying to hide his comings and goings anymore. He had even tricked himself into thinking that Czar wasn't thinking about him.

So he was completely taken by surprise when he found himself tied to a bed by two freaks he was trying to trick off with. He had met them at the mall and thought he was going to have the time of his life when they agreed to slide with him, but now his dream was turning into a nightmare.

"Y'all bitches betta untie me," he threatened. "I'm not playing," he added, trying to keep his panic down.

"Neither are we, Gauge," one of them said with a sneer. Her disgust for him was evident in every word.

He was shocked when he heard his name come out of her mouth because he never told them who he really was. In fact, he had been going by the tag GMoney since he had been back in the city. So to hear it roll off of her pretty lips with such disdain let him know that he was on a countdown. He tried to struggle against his bonds, but found himself tied securely. His last resort was begging and he tried to win an award for it. "Please let me go, I have kids. I'll give you a hundred bands to free me." The only response he received were laughs when he said something outrageous. He started to curse them out, but decided that it was pointless.

He must've dozed off because when he opened his eyes, there was Czar standing in between the two females, staring at him with an expressionless face. But he recognized the look in his eye and knew that he was about to die.

"Dior, Bianca, wait for me in the car," Czar ordered, speaking for the first time since laying eyes on Gauge.

Without a word, both ladies left the room to do as they were told. "Big homie, I——"

"You lost the right to call me that the moment you started hissing and turned snake," Czar growled angrily. Just the thought of his kin, one who he helped get off the streets, betraying him made his blood boil. "I started to kill your family one by one until you came out of hiding, but I decided against that because they weren't the ones who betrayed me. I knew you would pop up sooner or later, so I waited on you, and now here we are."

Gauge saw the rage in Czar's eyes, but he also saw the hurt, He should've never sided with Jimmy Slim, but his survival instinct led him wrong one time, and now he was going to pay for it. He sighed, but he refused to face death like he faced life, like a coward. "I have a hundred gee's stashed by the boat yards. Can you give that to my mother for my little brother and sister?"

Czar nodded his assent. He wouldn't deny his last request.

Gauge breathed a sigh of relief knowing that his family wouldn't starve without him around. "For what it's worth, big homie, I'm sorry for what I done. Now you can cleanse me from this earth for my betrayal." He held his chin up and locked eyes with Czar, ready to die.

Czar pulled his grave daggers and wished there were some way he could let him live, but the code he lived by wouldn't allow it. Betrayal had to be punished severely, and in this case, the price was death. He shot him in the chest one time because he wanted his mother to be able to recognize him when she buried him. He smirked as he left the crime scene because at the end, Gauge had showed a glimpse of the thoroughbred soldier he had the potential to be when he first met him. But just like Eve, he let the snake turn him, and for that, he had to die.

\*\*\*

King was staring at the group of young dudes standing in front of him, wondering if Tango was losing his marbles. By all accounts, they were vicious and getting to the bag, but you couldn't tell just by looking at them. They were all young, dressed in designer clothes, and carrying big guns they all had names for. They all repped North Carolina. But what made them rare was the fact that they all came from different cities and like most states, North

Cockit-back was just as territorial as any other, so to see the camaraderie between them was refreshing because the fastest way to end up in jail or somebody's graveyard was to deal with some niggas who wore masks. He liked the cocky little niggas because they gave off an energy that would fool an average Joe, but he saw their true nature. He would bet money that there was a lot of niggas buried somewhere because they underestimated them and thought they were soft. He looked over at Tango, who just chuckled.

"They are official, son," he said with a shrug of his shoulders.

"No disrespect to you or yours, but we don't need no one to vouch for us," Louie Lando, the unquestioned leader of this little band of misfits, said seriously. "We can make an example of fungus for you to let you know what it is," he added with strong eye contact.

King smirked because he respected him, but he was a little confused.

"Fungus is somebody you want removed because if left unchecked, it can contaminate the whole operation," Louie explained patiently.

"Introduce the rest of your team," King said, making his mind up.

Louie Lando was a part of a whole, so he nodded and let his people speak for themselves. "They call me Primo and I rep Fayette." He was 6'1", dark skin with locs. He had a big blunt in his mouth. He smoked nothing but Primo weed - hence the name.

"Pipe Down. I'm from Raleigh," a quiet-looking dude spoke up. He got his name because when he piped up, niggas piped down.

"Vicious. Enough said," a short, stocky nigga said with a smirk. "I'm from Charlotte."

"I'm Louie muthafuckin' Lando from Durham, a.k.a. Bull City, where we pop tops and dope spots," he said dramatically. The rest of his crew laughed at his antics. "We're called the Fly Committee," he added with flair.

"How are you eating now?" he asked curiously. Tango had told him a little bit, but he needed to know it from the horse's mouth.

Louie looked uncomfortable with the question because he knew that people wanted to know how he and his crew got their money so they could jump on the bandwagon, but their methods were only known to them, which kept informants guessing and police at bay. He looked to his crew to see how they felt. When they gave the go ahead, he felt better because he knew that they also realized the opportunity was frozen for them.

King peeped the move and respected them even more because it showed that they cared about each other and moved quietly despite how loud they seemed to be.

"We mostly scam, but we dibble and dabble in whatever can make us a quick profit," Louie finally answered.

King was intrigued, but kept it to himself for the time being. "So what makes you think you can handle the types of weight I'm dealing with?" he asked seriously. He needed to know that his product was making money and not collecting dust.

"Moving the product isn't a problem, but like I said before, we're scammers, so we're not trying to get locked into a long term deal. Feel me?" Louie knew that dope dealing wasn't for them because the potential for a quick profit big enough to finance their other moves was an opportunity too big to pass up. "We make money, you make money, and we part easily."

King prided himself on recognizing the strengths and weaknesses of the people he did business with, and the Fly Committee, as they fashioned themselves, were not drug dealers. So why place them in a position where they might fail? "I can see that you're only trying to finance your other projects by moving my weight, but that has the potential to go bad, and neither of us can afford that. Here's what I'm going to do for you though, I'm going to finance you on your scamming and you allow me to eat off of that plate also," he proposed

Louie looked at him skeptically, but he was intrigued. "So you will give us money to scam and you only want a percentage?" he asked dubiously. "Exactly," King replied with a smile. He found himself liking Louie more and more the longer they talked. "But I'm not talking about petty shit like getting clothes and shoes at the mall. If you are as good as you're portraying, then you have to make it worthwhile or why else do it, right?" he asked rhetorically.

"How much cash are we talking about, and what would you want back on your investment?" Louie asked seriously. He was now in business mode. "A million dollars to start, and you give me twenty percent off of every score from now on until we decide that our business is done." King knew that he was taking a gamble, but it was one he felt like could pay off big with little to no risk to him. "If you accept this money, then you fall under my family's umbrella until our business is done," he said seriously. "You will be allowed to operate however you see fit, but understand this, Louis Lando, Christopher Riley, Patrick Horn, Victor Owens... This will no longer be a game to pick up chicks and look fly. If what I've heard about you is even ten percent true, then I expect you to step your game up into the big leagues. No more swiping cards for shopping sprees unless it's worth it. If you accept what I'm offering, then you're on call and will be expected to show up if called upon. The rewards of aligning with me greatly outweigh the risks. So what is it going to be?"

Louie looked at the men he called his brothers and knew that they were shocked as he was to hear their government names come out of King's mouth. That just let them know that they were about to step into another world. But he could tell that they were excited about the come up. A million dollars would take their scams to another level and allow them to operate in a different tax bracket. Even though he had his reservations, it was too good of an opportunity to pass up.

He looked King in the eyes and smirked before he said, "How fast can we get that money?"

\*\*\*

Chaka was in love. She couldn't believe how much she had fallen for the Young Lion, but over the past year, he had shown time and time again that he was able to handle her and all of her baggage. She allowed herself to be open and in the process, let him do what no man had done before-know the real her. She showed him her demons and instead of running, he embraced her. That proved to her that he was a different kind of man. He knew that she had a past, but he did not question her. He allowed her actions to guide their relationship and it was liberating because he didn't get intimidated when she showed her strength. Sometimes she wondered if it turned him on because every time she challenged him, they would fuck like they were mad at each other. She kept telling herself that he was just something to do, something to get her mind off of killing, but the more time she spent in his presence, the more she never wanted to leave.

When one of her contacts called and informed her that Terror was found tied up in his kitchen with a bullet in his head, she reached out to her network and within the hour, she as studying the autopsy report and photos on her phone. Instantly she surmised that he was murdered by a professional. She couldn't explain exactly how she knew, but she didn't have any doubts about the method because she knew it so well. The job was clean and precise, but she didn't have any idea who Terror had pissed off enough other than herself. Now that Terror was out of the way, she focused her efforts on making sure his transition was a smooth one. She kept to the shadows, removing his more formidable enemies while he united the island. He never questioned her comings and goings, but when he demanded her presence, she never denied him. In the beginning, she never imagined him a part of her life for long, but that decision was now out of her hands

She stood in her bathroom waiting to see if she was with child, because if she was pregnant by the Young Lion, then their destinies would be intertwined forever. She started to pick up the pregnancy test she had just taken to see the results, but decide to wait another ten minutes just to be sure. This was already her fourth test because she had read about women having false positives, and she needed to be sure before she decided what to do. She still wasn't sure if she would tell her Young Lion about the pregnancy or get rid of it. She knew that once she told him that she was pregnant, all of her choices would disappear because he wouldn't allow her to even think about killing his chile.

With her anxiousness rising, she poked the test up and said a quick prayer before looking at the results. What she saw brought a smile to her face. Everything was going to be alright.

## CHAPTER 17

Raul walked out of the Dallas Federal detention center a different man. When he lost his father, something inside of him changed. It was like a part of him died when his father took his last breath. He felt responsible for his death in some ways because he brought Czar to his father, and Czar brought Jimmy Slim, and Jimmy Slim was attached to the snake who murdered him. He didn't know how he felt about Czar now. Even though he found out that he wasn't the rat, he still harbored the snitch Jimmy Slim in his camp. For years he had told Czar that something wasn't right with Jimmy, but he refused to listen to anything bad about him despite the obvious signs to everyone but him. Regardless of past friendships, whoever was remotely connected to his father's murder would be repaid in kind.

\*\*\*

Cha'nel was starting to get frustrated with her search for Chaka. It was like she had dropped off of the face of the earth. That made her unimaginably angry because it was like she was saying that her husband Rah'mel was so inconsequential that his death wouldn't garner any retaliation, but she would find out very soon just how wrong she was.

\*\*\*

"I understand, Gustav, but I'm no longer running the day to day... Yeah... You need to speak with King about any problem you have because I can't do anything for you." Sincere sighed as he hung up the phone. He looked up at Shinah with a worried expression on his face.

"Another one?" she asked, reading his expression. "These men do not like how King is running things." Sincere didn't have to guess about the repercussions of his son's actions because if he was the one being pushed out by some young boy, he would strike first and worry about the fallout after. He was seriously doubting if his son could run the pipeline he built and maintained for so many years. "We have to trust your sons to do what needs to be done and deal with any problems as they arise," Shinah said seriously. She was also worried about her children, but she also understood that they had little choice in what they did until they were in a better position to make their move and when they moved, they needed to be strong.

"These men are killers," Sincere said seriously. "They are a part of the Council, albeit, low level, but they are still powerful in their own right. To be pushed out or stripped of that power by someone they feel is beneath them is gasoline to the fire, and the only way to ensure the safety of our family is to erase these men from the board." He was starting to regret letting Royalty force him to retire because now he was beginning to miss the hustle and grind of controlling men and money.

Shinah smirked at him because he sounded like a grumpy old man with nothing to do. He didn't like retirement at all.

"What?" he exclaimed when he saw the smirk on her face.

"You just miss the grind." she replied teasingly. Sincere sighed because what she said was true, "I do miss it, love, but I wouldn't miss it as much if I felt that we were in control of the outcome," he said passionately. "I just feel like we're puppets in someone's play," he added angrily.

"You have to realize that we can only control ourselves," she said seriously. "We have to be prepared for whatever outcome that happens. Instead of you being salty, you need to make yourself useful to your sons and give them whatever they need to remain safe." She looked at him and shook her head. She was contemplating whether or not to reveal all that she knew about the Council of Kings because she knew a lot more than she let on. She was not without her own connections and resources. But she had to be careful on how much she revealed because here greatest weapon of all was her ability to seem non-threatening

Sincere was watching Shinah and realized that he didn't know everything she had been through anymore. She was a lot more serious than he remembered and a lot more cautious. His feelings were still there, but for some strange reason, he knew that he didn't have to protect her anymore. "You're right, we have to take care of our own," he said quietly. "When the time comes, we just have to be ready."

***

Gustav hung up his phone and looked at the men arrayed in front of him. His complexion was reddened from the intense anger he was feeling after his conversation with Sincere. He knew a dismissal when he heard one, and it pissed him off. He's been a soldier his whole life and he understood the chain of commands and hierarchies with the best of them, especially when it came to the Council of Kings. So he refused to be pushed to the bottom of the food chain by some unproven neophyte, no matter who his father was. To him, it seemed like there wasn't any stability at the top of the totem pole and where chaos reigned, opportunity present itself. He looked at his men and smiled.

"Prepare for war, boys. We're about to start getting a bigger slice of pie."

***

Chaka was losing her mind. She was actually browsing for baby clothes in a specialty shop and was actually enjoying it. She wasn't thinking about targets and head shots. She was thinking about baby diapers, children's clothes, and late nights with no sleep. She didn't even know how Majestic felt about kids or having kids with her, but she really didn't care either because she knew that he would get with the program. Her life wasn't cookie cutter enough for a kid, but she knew that God didn't make mistakes, so she would accept whatever blessings he gave her and adapt because Majestic made her feel like she could merge both of her worlds——assassin and mother.

***

Cha'nel was doing reconnaissance in downtown Miami when her sixth sense went off, alerting her to danger in her immediate surroundings. She immediately surveyed the pedestrians swirling around her and didn't sense what her brain knew was an apex predator. She continued to scan for the threat as she walked past the store after store. As she was passing the display window to the baby store, she felt her pulse quicken when she finally laid eyes on the woman who had altered her universe. Her visceral need for revenge had her temporarily forgetting her train because she was rooted in place, gawking at Chaka, who appeared to be shopping for a child, but she didn't put too much stock in appearances because her target might be on a job.

A passing pedestrian bumped into her as he walked by, jarring her from the murderous trance she was currently in. With her training back in control, she forced her feet to move, but she kept her eyes on her prey as she crossed the street to remain unseen. She watched Chaka like a hawk: her mannerisms, every eye blink, smile and flip of her hair. What had her undivided attention was the way Chaka kept placing her left hand protectively over her stomach. Was she really pregnant? she thought curiously. It seemed farfetched that someone in their profession would purposely have a child knowing the risks it would bring to them from their enemies. She kept watching because with everything she had learned about Chaka, this could very well be an elaborate ruse. If this was what Chaka was doing, then it would indicate that she knew she was being stalked for death, and if that was the case then she could be setting up the kill box for her.

Cha'nel cursed as she extinguished her anger because it would get her killed if she didn't rein it in. She moved to a coffee shop across the street so she could keep an eye on her prey. She had a decision to make. Would she just kill Chaka, or would she kill the baby too?

## CHAPTER 18

Scales woke up disoriented. He blinked a few times to clear his eyes, but he couldn't see anything because his surroundings were pitch black. He shook his head to dislodge the cobwebs clouding his mind. He tied to remember exactly what had happened the last twenty-four hours, but he couldn't. He started panicking when he tried to stand up and found himself tied to a chair. His fear of what was happening to him quickly cleared his mind and helped him remember how he had gotten into his current situation. When King took over for Sincere, he was one of the few who saw it as an opportunity to level up and he disregarded the new order, thinking that nothing would come for his insubordination. But he was how tie to a chair in a room so dark that he couldn't see six inches in front of him.

"Pussy bwoy, ye wanta play games wit' mem money?"

Scales was confused but also a little relieved because King was a New York nigga and the voice talking to him was definitely Jamaican. As far as he knew, he didn't have any problems with any Jamaicans, so he was sure that he could clear up the obvious misunderstanding they had brewing. "My man, I think you have the wrong man tied up here," he said confidently. "Just untie me and I'll forgive you for your disrespect," he added threateningly.

"Ye de wrong man, ye say?"

"Damn right." Scales was growing more confident by the minute. The longer he stayed alive, the more he felt like he was winning.

"Okay, mon."

Scales breathed a sigh of relief because it seemed as if he had convinced his assailant that he had the wrong man and as soon as he was untied, he could add to his body count. Niggas would learn real quick about the consequences for fucking with him.

Suddenly the light were cut on, forcing him to close his eyes until he was able to adjust to the blinding brightness. When he opened them again, he was hit with a wave of confusion at the sight in front of him. He violently shook his head, hoping that he was hallucinating, but the image remained unchanged causing him to wonder if he had been drugged. Maybe this was hell, he thought fearfully. "Scales, Scales, Scales," King said pitifully. He looked down at the man in disgust. No matter how much you tried to help people, greed always caused someone to test you and when that happened, you made an example out of them, hence Scales being tied to a chair in an empty warehouse... "you thought you could play with my money and I wouldn't find out?" he asked seriously. "King, I swear to God I'm not playing with your bread, cuz," Scales pleaded with wide eyes as he continued looking back and forth between King and his mirror images standing shoulder to shoulder with him.

"So many of you fuck niggas say the same shit after you've been caught. Shut the fuck up, young'un, and man up," Czar growled at the sniffling man. "Bitch ass."

"Can we hurry this up?" Pharaoh joked. "We have shit to do later on."

"King, I swear to God, on my mama and my kids, I did not play with your money!" Scales cried as he realized that his death was imminent.

Czar scoffed in disgust as he pulled his grave diggers and shot Scales in the chest.

Scales looked down at the gaping hole in his chest and felt this life flowing out of his body. "Oh God. Oh God. Oh God." He felt like he was hyperventilating.

Czar walked over to his latest victim and whispered in his ear. "God is there," he said, pointing towards the sky with one of his grave diggers. "I'm down here and you crossed the wrong nigga," he added before putting a bullet in his head.

Majestic looked at Czar and narrowed his eyes. "Ye stole mem kill, brudda," he growled playfully. Czar looked at his brother and smirked. "Ye ladies are playing wut yer food," he said, mocking his accent. "I just ate mine."

"We're almost done sewing things up," King said seriously. "The push back has been a little more aggressive than we expected, but we've been able to put out every fire because we've done it together." "Are you sure that getting the attention of the people at the top is the way to go?" Pharaoh asked dubiously. He wasn't sure if they were ready to ruffle the feathers of the top Council members, but he would do his part whether he agreed or not. "It's the only way we can gain control of our destinies," King said to his brothers. "Our good ol' auntie is not being sincere as far as her plans for us. We are in a position to make our own demands and solidify our spot. Why do you think we're pushing these niggas out?" he asked rhetorically. "If the operation is completely ours, then it can't be run without us. I don't know about you, but I'm not out here putting my life on the line to catch crumbs off of someone else's plate." He made sure to make eye contact with each of his brothers before moving on. "This is a different league we're playing in and there's only two outcomes to this game: success or death."

"None of this is a coincidence," Czar said, taking the reins from King. "We're seeing more paper than ever, but if we don't complete the mission, it can and probably will be taken away from us. Anybody not rocking to our beat will be put to sleep," he finished adamantly.

"We 'ave de whole island wit' us," Majestic informed them. It had taken hard work and more than a little bloodshed to get Jamaica under his country but it was a price he was willing to pay to keep his word to Buju. At first he tried to play the sidelines and make things better for his people, but he quickly realized he wasn't built for the administrative duties required for the job. So he handed over the day to day to his sisters with Nicholas advising them and jumped back into the field with his brothers and his Rude Bwoy crew. "How are you doing on your end, bro?" King asked Pharaoh, who was in charge of legitimizing them and acquiring political clout in case they were ever jammed up beyond norm.

"Well-placed bribes have gained us access to some notable power, but I'm still working on some moves that will bulletproof us legally and illegally. We will be okay with time." Pharaoh knew how important his success was to his brothers and was determined not to fail.

"Now that that's settled, let's roll the rest of these old timers and make sure those in the know think twice before coming for us," Czar said, ready to paint the town red.

"Well said, bro," King said with a smirk. "Let's get to it."

\*\*\*

Raul was starting to become frustrated because he still wanted to find out the identity of the person who killed his father. For some inexplicable reason, his father had cut his camera feeds and sent this security team away every time this person was in his presence, which let him know that it was a woman - one who had entirely too much influence over his father. What confused him still was why his father hid her from him, something he never did before. He was well aware of his father's affinity for bedding his rivals significant others, despite how many times he warned him about the lunacy of doing so, so he wondered who she belonged to. They had to be influential to make his father proceed with caution when they were a Council member. He started to question his father's motives. Surely his father did not cross that line. Either way, he was no closer to finding the person responsible for his father's death than when he was in prison. The only thing left for him to do was go see the only person left alive who could possibly connect the dots for him. It was time to face Czar.

## CHAPTER 19

Regina Lopez loved helping people. She had been doing it since she was a little girl and it was the main reason she got into nursing. She had been working at Miami General Hospital for half her life and at forty-four years old, she didn't plan on returning anytime soon. She loved the hustle and bustle of nursing. She loved her patients and they adored her because she went above and beyond for them. She was always at the hospital making sure things ran smoothly and she enjoyed it, loving the career she chose for herself.

But while her professional life was on an upward trajectory, her personal life couldn't be in more disarray. It seemed as if she attracted every cheater in Florida because without fail, no matter how good the relationship was going, they cheated on her. She considered herself a good woman. She cooked, she was supportive, and she even stepped out of her comfort zone and took a pole dancing class to spice up here sex life, but nothing worked because she kept getting cheated on. So she threw herself into her work losing herself in the constant needs of her patients.

Over the course of her career, she had seen hundreds of odd cases, but none ever intrigued her more than normal until she was put in charge of a John Doe patient who was supposed to be very dangerous. At first he had constant police presence guarding him despite the fact that he was in a coma, but after months of no change in his condition, the police presence grew smaller and smaller until they decided that John Doe did not warrant that many man hours they called weekly asking for updates, then monthly, until eventually they also stopped. But she never stopped taking care of him. The doctors even gave up any hope of him ever regaining consciousness, but she still went about her duties like he was just asleep instead of in a coma. As the weeks, then months, went by, she felt like she got to know the unknown man better than anyone she had ever dated before. She held conversations with him as she groomed him. He listened to all of her problems without judgment and she actually felt like he could hear her. When she gave him his sponge baths, she memorized every muscle and scar on his body. She had never known a man in better shape. It seemed to her as if he worked out every day. As the time went by she became attached to the John Doe, She had even given him a name. She called him Miguel. If she was being truthful to herself, she had fallen in love with him, and he had never said a word to her. She confided her secrets, wants, and designs to him. She told him about her childhood and about all the bad choices she had made in men. She had even come to appreciate their one-sided conversations because she felt free from judgment. She even became possessive and territorial when it came to her John Doe. She wouldn't let any other nurse take care of him in any way, so she was at the hospital every chance she could get, and if she had to leave for any reason at all, she would return as soon as he was able. For hours on end she talked to him about the life they were going to have together as soon as he woke up. In her mind, it was the best relationship she had ever had and for all intents and purposes, he was her man. She wouldn't let anyone come between them. Period!

*\*\*\**

Javier looked at his daughter with contempt and disgust. He was a chauvinistic pig, one who didn't believe that a woman was good for anything besides fucking and cooking, in that exact order, but the women standing in front of him with an expression on her face that matched his was challenging him in ways no woman had ever dreamed of doing. It was pissing him off to no end that he needed her to achieve his goals, but he did. So he would tolerate her until he didn't need her anymore and then he would finally wash his hands of her by doing what he should've done the day she was born: kill her. "Update," he ordered angrily.

Royalty smirked as she looked at her father because she knew how much he hated needing her, but she also knew that when he no longer found her useful that he would try to kill her, and she had no doubt whatsoever that her usefulness would soon run out. Before that happened, she needed to make sure that all her pieces were in place, so when she made sure that all the pieces were in place and made her move, she would be the last one standing. Satisfied that she was prepared for any eventual outcome, she gave her report and waited while he gave her the information.

"That's very good, because the Council has taken notice," he said, ecstatic with the way his plans were coming together. "A meeting had been called for the North American sector of the Council. That is where I will petition the Council to allow Mexico to become a part of North America. This will allow me to eventually take over Bobby's territory personally instead of by proxy. So I need you to make sure that there are no complications on your end because I will not allow you to make me look stupid in front of the

Council." He made sure she knew what the consequences would be if she failed.

Royalty resisted the urge to roll her eyes. "You're representing me and I won't allow you to make me look stupid in front of the Council," he said seriously.

"You know, Father, that's the second time you've said that," she said with a smirk.

Javier was about to cuss at her until he realized that's exactly what she was goading him to do. "Dismissed," he said with a sneer.

Royalty locked eyes with her father for a few seconds before turning on her heels and walking out. She was now on a countdown, and she couldn't afford for it to run out.

Javier waited a minute after the door closed behind his loathsome daughter before pressing a button situated under his desk. He smiled at the man who walked into his room through a side door, almost invisible to the naked eyes. "You heard everything that was said?" he asked the man.

"Everything. When will you be ready?" he asked curiously.

"Is everything ready on your end?" Javier asked, ignoring the man's question. He didn't want the man to think he could question anything he did. The hierarchy was established and wouldn't change anytime soon.

"I will be in full control before the new moon sits in the sky."

"Good, because we can't afford any slip- ups," Javier said quietly. "In this game of life and death, one false move can be the end of you." He eyed the man in front of him in disgust. "Just make sure you are because I will tie up all loose ends," he added threateningly.

"Everything's in order. Don't worry," the man replied, bristling at the implied threat.

"It better be," Javier said casually. "When we're secure, you can have your revenge on my daughter. You will be doing me a favor so I hope you succeed, for your sake," he said with a smirk. "Until then, stay ready. Dismissed," he added, giving his attention to some miscellaneous paperwork on his desk.

Moses smiled and let the disrespect roll off of his back like water on a duck. He knew that he would have the last laugh in the end. He made his exit through the same door he entered through because he had plans to make and bodies to catch.

Javier looked up when he heard the door close and saw that his accomplice was gone. He was hit with a sudden wave of doubt when he thought about the plan he was trying to implement because he had to trust others outside of his immediate circle, which consisted of him, God, and sometimes the devil, depending on his mood. With so many moving parts it was damn near impossible not to have lines pop up. He just hoped that they weren't big enough to consume him and everything he had worked his whole life for.

*** 

Bianca and Dior were now the boss bitches they were always meant to be. After Czar had reestablished his name everywhere Jimmy Slim tarnished it, he kept his word and bought them the old strip club they used to dance at. It had taken a lot of hard work and sacrifice on both of their parts, but they had accomplished what they set out to do. In just under a year, the five star club was the hottest night spot in Dallas, Texas. They had the sexiest women in the south dancing on their stages. Celebrities regularly frequented their establishment, who in turn brought out the biggest money-getters in the city to try and outshine them It wasn't unusual to see a half a million dollars raining down on ass and titties on any given night. It was an upscale club where men came to have a good time and the private rooms started at ten thousand dollars an hour. Simply put, it was the place to see and be seen!

Czar was sitting in the back in one of the V.I.P. lounges, waiting for his former friend Raul to show up. He really didn't have a problem with him, but his father did try to have him removed from this world. So that slid him out of the friend category and firmly into the associate lane. The club didn't open up for a few more hours, as they would have plenty of privacy to wash out whatever it was Raul had on his chest. He had thought about postponing the meeting because he didn't know how it was going to turn out and he didn't like unknowns, but he granted the meeting face to face, hoping that Raul wanted to discuss business. He didn't know how it would go if he wanted to talk about Martinez.

He looked up when he felt a presence standing at the entrance to the lounge he was sitting in. He smiled when he saw Dior standing there.

Dior couldn't help the smile that blossomed onto her. Face when Czar smiled at her. She loved him so much that it made her happy just to see him. She walked over and straddled his lap. She looked into his eyes and saw that he was worried about something.

"You think you can read me."

"Like the back of my hand," she replied sassily. "You're worried about your meeting?" she asked softly.

Czar thought about her question for a few seconds before shaking his head. "I'm just wondering what his mindset will be because if it's in any way aggressive, then I'm going to slump him," he said seriously. "Hopefully it won't come to that because he will understand or be the cause of his own demise."

Dior was about to respond until she heard someone clear their throat behind them. She turned and saw Bianca standing at the

148

doorway with a handsome Hispanic man standing beside her. She slid off of Czar's lap and walked over to Bianca. She took her hand and left the lounge, closing the door behind them.

Czar watched Raul trying to get a read on him, trying to see what the mood was, but he was a stone wall. He stood up and held his hand out because he wanted to start the meeting off with no hostility. He would let Raul move them in whatever direction they would go. "You picked up some weight in jail," he joked when they shook hands. "Had a lot of time on my hands," Raul said with a straight face.

Guess it won't be friendly, Czar thought sardonically. "What's on your mind?" he asked seriously. All traces of humor are gone from his voice.

"Finding everyone involved in my father's death," Raul said, seeing no point in wasting time or words.

"Whoever killed your father did me a favor because I would've done it myself for his transgression against my life," Czar said seriously. Raul had set the tone and he would dance to the beat.

Raul's emotions flared at his word, but he reined them in because he knew that Czar's reputation was well-earned and now wasn't the time to move recklessly. Everything in due time. He took a deep breath and let it out slowly before speaking again. "My father was being manipulated by whoever killed him and can't be blamed for his actions," he said calmly.

Czar looked at Raul like he had grown two heads. He couldn't believe what he was actually saying. "I don't give a fuck who was pulling his strings," he fumed. "He tried to end my life with some bullshit. There's no coming back from that. He didn't even have the courtesy to have a sit down with me to find out if it was true." He scoffed at the idea of forgiving Martinez for his actions. "I hope he enjoyed that pussy, because he got smoked because of it," he added sarcastically.

Raul looked at Czar sharply. "Why do you think it was a woman who killed my father?" he asked suspiciously. He had his own theories about his father's death, but even he wasn't positive it was a woman, so Czar hinting that it might be a female had him alert.

Czar smirked because Raul thought that he was smarter than him, but he had him right where he wanted him, chasing his own tail. "I never crossed Martinez or gave him cause to be suspicious of me because I'm ten toes down no matter the situation. I'm no fucking rat." He paused and took a deep breath before his anger over took him because he still saw red whenever he thought about the attempted assassination of his hard-earned name.

Raul felt a change in Czar's energy immediately and knew that things could go left in an instant. So he kept his peace and warily watched for any sudden movements that could spell his end. "So for your father to push the button on me and then back Jimmy Slim told me that he was blinded by some good pussy. There are only two types of people in this world who move like that." "And what are those?" Raul asked angrily. He knew Czar was going to disrespect his father, but there was nothing he could do about it at that moment besides eat it and let it fuel his need for revenge.

"Boys and suckas," Czar said seriously. "Only you know which category your father falls into" He locked eyes with Raul to let him know what he thought of his father: nothing at all.

Raul felt his anger curse through his body and abruptly stood up. He would no longer sit and listen to someone who wasn't fit to tie his father's shoes disrespect their family. He locked eyes with Czar and spoke with certainty. "Believe me when I tell you this, Czar: whoever was connected to my father will be hunted down and killed in the most horrifying ways. Trust me on that."

Czar also stood up and made sure his eyes never left the man he was sure he would have to kill one day soon. "Be careful pulling on that thread, Raul," he said calmly. "You might end up getting choked with it."

Raul maintained eye contact for a few sec-
onds as he digested the threat he just received, then he abruptly spun on his heel and left the lounge without another word.

Czar stared after him and wondered if he had made a mistake letting Raul leave the club alive. He shrugged his shoulders and put it in the back of his mind. He just hoped that if it was a mistake that he could be the one to pay for it and not anyone he loved.

## CHAPTER 20

Cha'nel had a serious dilemma on her hands. Chaka, her arch enemy, was pregnant, and she didn't know what to do. As a rule she never killed kids. In fact, she and Rah'mel usually ended up killing any client who wanted them to kill a child because they felt like children were protected by God and you would quickly meet your end if you hurt one of his flock. But the one carrying this child murdered the love of her life. She was fighting herself trying to decide what to do. On one hand she figured that she could wait until the child was born and then kill Chaka at her weakest moment, but as fast as that thought entered her mind she dismissed it because she wasn't a coward. She wanted to honor her love by earning her kill, so that option was out. On the other hand, she wanted to exact her revenge despite the child and face the consequences of God and Rah'mel whenever she took her last breath, which she expected to shortly happen after Chaka took hers. She wasn't naive enough to think that she would leave that fight to the death unscathed. She fully expected to die from the wounds she was sure she would sustain from Chaka. Rah'mel was superior to her in every way when it came to combat so if Chaka was able to take him down, then she would expect her death also, but she would make sure Chaka followed her to the afterlife.

Ever since she had found her prey shopping for baby clothes she had used all of her surveillance training to follow her around the city. It was surprisingly easy. Chaka seemed caught up in her impending pregnancy and not as locked into her training as she should be. She knew all of her usual haunts but until she figured out her conflicting emotions concerning the child, she would just watch and wait, something she wasn't that good at.

*** 

Eric Smith was nothing much to look at physically. He was 5'8" in height, 160 pounds, and as pale as a man who's scared of the sun, but he was one of the smartest people on the planet. By the age of sixteen he had three doctorates and two multimillion dollar companies, which he sold because it was too easy. Running a company with hundreds of employees who all did the exact right thing was boring for him. So he took all of his profits from the sales of these companies and started his journey into the criminal underworld.

He went about his task just like he would any legal endeavor. He did his research, figured out the risk, and came up with a plan that would offer him the least amount of exposure and maximum profits. The more he studied past criminal organizations, the more he realized that all of their failures boiled down to one common mistake: too much exposure. For some odd reason, criminals felt the need to show off their ill-gotten gains to the less fortunate, and the need to rub it in the authorities' faces was something he could never understand. But he learned from their mistakes continuously as he built his legend. Anonymity was his greatest weapon because it allowed him to move in between two worlds without notice. He knew that he wouldn't be able to physically intimidate his way to where he wanted to be, so he used the intelligence God blessed him with. He used people just as one would use toilet tissue. He threw them away after whatever task he assigned them was completed. Some of them he kept around longer to act as his proxy in his illegal dealings. He let him play boss while he controlled the actions of his puppet, thus controlling whatever illegal activity he chose to participate in.

He was content with his little piece of the pie until he was approached by a secret organization called the Council of Kings. At first he refused to believe that someone, anyone, knew who he was and what he had been up to over the last deceased, but they quickly dispelled the notion that he had about anonymity. They showed him that he was only invisible to people not powerful enough to see through the bullshit, and they showed him exactly who he was. They broke him down, made him feel like his old weak self, something he hadn't felt in over a decade, but they offered to build him up, put him in a position to be what he really wanted to be: one of the biggest criminals in the world with complete anonymity. Except from them, of course. They gave him a week to think over their offer and he got the feeling that no wasn't going to be acceptable answer.

So he took the allotted time and tried to find out who these people were, but even with all of his connections, he couldn't find so much as a whisper about them. He felt a tinge of fear but he mostly felt excitement about the opportunity to extend his reach and play the game on a global scale. He knew that he was being underestimated, and he would use that to his advantage to move until he was sitting at the top of the food chain. He was now the cochain of North America and he had plans to continue his ascent to the top very soon, but at the moment, he had pressing matters that needed attending to.

His phone rang, causing him to grimace as he answered. "Hello...What is it?" He listened to one of his subordinates fill him in on one of his more pressing matters. "Set up a meeting with all the pertinent parties involved. If violations are found, then they will be handled, but make sure anyone who has the slightest involvement is present. Do not disappoint me." He hung up and sighed because some new players were introducing themselves to the game. He had a feeling that things were about to get real interesting.

\*\*\*

Nurse Lopez was tending to her man, telling him about some of her disrespectful coworkers and how they were whispering about how much she gave him, when she felt his fingers move. Startled, she jumped back with her heart hammering inside of her chest as she watched his body waking itself up. She realized that by doing so she would be sending her soulmate to jail and that was something she couldn't fathom. She walked back over to his bed and watched his vitals to make sure nothing happened that she couldn't handle herself. A plan formed in her mind. She didn't want to notify anyone that he was waking up. She grabbed his hand and massaged it as she continued to watch his vitals. She was taking deep breaths to calm herself down because she was on the verge of hyper-ventilating, and she couldn't afford for anything to close her mind as she prepared to jeopardize her will being and her freedom.

She bent down and started whispering into his ear as she continued to massage his hand, hoping that he was actually hearing her as she talked to him over the past year. Her only chance of success was if he woke up and knew her. Her breath caught in her throat when she saw his eyelids fluttering. He opened his eyes and immediately closed them again as the light stung his senses. When he felt that he could stand to open them without tearing up, he did, and the first thing he saw was a beautiful nurse standing there crying. He tried to talk, but the trachea tube in his throat prevented him from doing so. Regina looked at the man she had fallen in love with and knew that she was standing on the precipice of a lifealtering decision. On one hand, she was jeopardizing her freedom and her life, but on the other hand, she had an opportunity to find true happiness. Her decision was made when she saw the recognition in his eyes as tears flowed down his cheeks. She slowly removed the tube from his throat and fed him some ice chips until he was finally able to at least whisper some words.

"Mi amor Regina," he pushed out with extreme effort.

Regina was so happy because all of her dreams were coming true, but she had one last task to complete before she could live her dream life: killing him.

## CHAPTER 21

Majestic was staring at Chaka with an expression on his face that she couldn't read and she was becoming anxious. She had just told him that she was pregnant and was extremely nervous about what his reaction would be. Anyone who knew her would say that she was acting out of character, but she couldn't seem to be able to help herself. For the first time in her life, she loved something other than the kill and she would do anything to hold onto that love, even if that meant having his baby, which was a no-no in her profession. She was just starting to get frustrated with his silence when he spoke.

"Ave ye been ta de doctor?" he asked seriously.

She frowned at him because to her ears, it was as if he was doubting her, and that pissed her off to no end. If he only understood how much she was risking by having his baby, then he wouldn't question her at all.

Majestic smirked because he saw that she was about to erupt. Her fire was one of the things he loved about her, that and the fact that she wasn't scared of him. It was refreshing after having everyone bow down to you all the time and now she was giving him a priceless gift. It was only right that he give her something of equal value: himself. He took her hand and got down on one knee.

Chaka gasped when she saw him one on one knee staring up at her with that smirk she found so irritating sometimes. "What are you doing?" she asked quietly. She hated how shaky her voice sounded, which alerted her that tears were on the way.

Majestic finally let his smirk bloom into a full smile as he looked into the eye of the woman he wanted to spend the rest of his life with. "Loving ye," he replied happily. "Will ye do mem de 'onor of being mem wife?" he asked seriously.

Chaka tried to answer, but choked on her words as the tears started flowing down her cheeks, so she just nodded her head yes before grabbing him up and kissing him.

"Mem don't 'ave a ring but mem 'ope dis will do in the meantime." He pulled the lion's head necklace over his head and placed it around her neck.

Chaka grasped the lion's head in her hand, feeling the power it contained. She was in awe because she knew what the necklace meant to him. In that moment, she didn't have any regrets. She was truly happy.

*** 

Shinah hung up the phone after talking to her sister and looked at Sincere, who was watching her intently. "Why are you looking at me like that?" she asked with an arched eyebrow.

"I'm sitting here wondering how long it will take me to get you out of those clothes," he answered with a smile.

Over the last year they had picked back up like they hadn't been separated for over twenty years. It hadn't been without its hiccups - mainly Moses in his feelings about the kids - but other than that, things had been going well.

Shinah chuckled at him, but slowly stopped. The phone call she just had with Royalty wouldn't allow her to think about anything but that. "As much as I would love to find out, we're going to have to put that on the back burner because we have more pressing matters at hand to deal with."

"Who was that on the phone?" he asked as he got his mind back on business.

"Royalty."

Sincere grimaced because whenever she was involved, trouble usually followed in her wake. "What did she want?"

"We've been summoned," Shinah said as a bad feeling invaded her body.

"By who?" Sincere asked, adopting her energy.

"The Council," she replied simply.

Sincere frowned because even though he expected it, it happened a lot faster than he thought. Their sons were really shaking things up if they were already attracting the attention of the Council. "What did she say this was about?" he asked seriously.

Shinah sighed because she knew that her answers were frustrating him, but it was all she had to give. "She didn't know, but said to be ready for anything," she said with a frown.

"Call the boys and tell them to get their affairs in order," Sincere said as he stood up. He had to make some calls to see if he could get some clarity about this meeting. He didn't like walking into anything blindly. "Also, call Royalty back and tell her that whatever her plan is, it better work, because if we die, so will she," he added coldly before leaving the room.

Shinah was apprehensive about this summons because there were too many unknowns. She looked at the door Sincere had just walked through and realized that everything she loved was in danger. She picked the phone back up and dialed a number that she thought she would never use again. It was time to use her ace in the hole.

***

Nurse Lopez was terrified about what she was attempting to do. Since Miguel had regained consciousness, she had been consumed with thoughts of him going to prison, and that was something she couldn't allow to happen. She had been sleeping, eating, and showering at the hospital since he had awoken to make sure that no one accidentally discovered that he was out of his coma and report it to the authorities, but also to try and come up with a plan to get her man home. Ironically, the idea she was able to come up with to accomplish her goal came from an old pervert who had been hitting on her since she started working there. She had never entertained his advances or taken him seriously because she wasn't attracted to him at all. He was white and she didn't do pink meat, but once she found out from him that a part of his job was signing death certificates, she made up her mind to make him an unwitting accomplice to her plans. Before going down to his office, she did her makeup and put on her tightest nurse uniform because she needed him thinking with the smaller of his two heads if she was to pull this off. She was getting a lot of looks on her way to the elevator and that let her know that she was looking good in her uniform. As she descended to his office, she wiped her palm against her thighs repeatedly because she was becoming increasingly more nervous the closer she got to his floor. When the elevator doors opened up, she got to his floor. She hesitated getting off and thought about finding a different way, but knew that she didn't have the time because at any moment, her ruse could be discovered and she couldn't afford for that to happen. She took a deep breath and stepped off of the elevator. When she arrived at the right office, she took another deep breath before knocking on the door.

"Nurse Lopez, what a pleasant surprise," Doctor Gunter exclaimed when he opened his door and saw her face. His stare was lecherous as he looked her up and down.

"Hey Stephen," she replied nervously. He made her uncomfortable with his salacious behavior.

"So what brings you to my humble abode?" he asked with a small smile when he saw that he had her squirming.

"Uh, I need your signature for something real quick," she said with what she hoped was a sexy smile on her face.

Stephan eyed her for a second before stepping to the side and letting into his office. His suspicious nature was in overdrive as he thought about all of the instances she went out of her way to avoid him, but now here she was asking for a favor with a smile on her face. Maybe I've worn her down, he thought as he locked his office door and made sure no one could see through the blinds. "So what is it that needs my signature?" he asked hopefully. He was eager to be of assistance and win some brownie points with her.

"With this," she said before handing him the paperwork.

"This is a death certificate," he said after looking over everything she gave him. He looked at her with confusion on his face. "Why are you the one bringing me this?" he asked suspiciously.

Regina inadvertently wiped her palms against her thighs, drawing Stephen's eyes to her unusually tight uniform, because the way he was looking at her was making her nervous and it was causing her hands to sweat. She had to come up with a believable lie quickly before her plan blew up in her face. She took yet another deep breath and gave him her best smile. "You know how busy it gets up there and how I'm the one who always wants to help out anyway I can," she said, adding a sheepish look for good measure.

"So can you sign this paperwork?" she sked, grimacing at the hopeful lilt in her voice.

"I don't know about this, Nurse Lopez," he said dubiously.

Regina felt her heart stop as her hopes shattered with every word out of his mouth. She felt like she was about to have a panic attack.

"Unless you're willing to give me what I want," he said anxiously. He saw the panicky look on her face when she thought he wouldn't help her, so he decided to see if he could leverage her desperation into what he wanted. Fair exchange was no robbery.

Regina was still wallowing in her self-pity party, trying to come up with a new plan, when Stephen started talking, so she only caught the end. It didn't make any sense to her, so she asked him to repeat himself. When he did and she heard exactly what he said, she snapped. "What!" she exclaimed angrily. She was looking at him like was looking at him like he was the scum of the earth. "I knew that you were a pig, but this is low even for you," she fumed.

Stephen was confused because he had been sure that he had her pegged right this time, but her anger made him pause and question if he was that far off target. He didn't think so, but he wasn't certain. He decided to push her as far as she would allow and if he was wrong, he could be jeopardizing his livelihood, all because he wanted some pussy. "Well, I think I should call upstairs and verify what you're asking me to do," he bluffed as he picked up the phone and started dialing numbers. He held his breath and hoped that he was right because he really couldn't afford not to be.

Regina's eyes grew wide with fright when she saw him dialing upstairs. With each number he pushed, she saw her dream life disappearing. She rushed over and pressed the dial tone button with a nervous smile gracing her lips. "There's no need to get anyone else involved, Stephen," she said in a shaky voice.

Stephen slowly replaced the phone back into the base and silently released the breath he had been holding as a feeling of euphoria washed over him. He looked in her eyes and realized that he had her in the palm of his hand, ready to do whatever he demanded she do. "Are you ready to give me what I want for my signature?" he asked just to be sure they were both on the same page.

Regina felt like crying, but she fought them back because she refused to let him see her breakdown. She nodded her head, giving her assent.

Stephen finally let his smile blossom onto his face at his victory. He felt himself get an erection and was ready to get out. "Suck my dick, and go slow," he ordered forcefully. "I don't want to cum too quickly."

Regina started to protest, but bit her tongue when she remembered the bigger picture. She would do anything to make her dreams into a reality. She looked into his eyes as she slowly sank to her knees and knew that he was going to get his money's worth. She just hoped that there was enough left of her soul to make sense of all that was sacrificed.

***

Moses was happy to be home. Nigeria was where he grew into a man, where he learned about his true self, but he had a love-hate relationship with his country. He loved the camaraderie and openness of the people of his birth country. It was the exact opposite of the blacks of America. But he also hated the oppressive ideology of his people, the restrictive thinking and the rigid customs. His father was a combination of everything he hated about his homeland. He was a disciplinarian and as his only child, he bore the brunt of his anger. For some reason, he couldn't seem to do anything right in his father's eyes and he didn't have any qualms about showing his displeasure in private or public. He grew up resenting his father, but that didn't stop him from seeking his approval every chance he got.

The closer he got to his father's compound, the more the feeling of inadequacy invaded his body. He hated coming home, but this time it was necessary because he couldn't complete his plans without his father's help. When his chauffeured SUV rolled through the gates of the estate, he felt like he was having a panic attack. He did everything in his power to calm himself down before one of the guards saw him and reported his weakness to his father. Once he was finally under control, he climbed out of the SUV and made his way into the main house. Every guard he passed stood at attention, but he knew it was all for show because his father despised him and they followed his every emotion, so they despised him also.

As he made his way toward his father's wing of the house he was surprised he didn't run into Abdul, his father's most trusted advisor. They hated each other and made no secret about it. Abdul wanted to run the Bandele family after his father passed, but because he wasn't family, it would never happen, and it ate at him from the inside out. So Abdul took every opportunity to belittle and undermine him in front of his father and the family. Normally he would have had him beheaded a long time ago, but because of his standing with his father, he was untouchable. He bided his time because he knew that as soon as his father died, he could be head of the family and Abdul would finally meet his fate at the chopping block.

He arrived at his father's door and paused to gather himself before knocking. He knew that he had to be on his toes because his father never missed an opportunity to get under his skin. Before he could knock, the door opened and Samuel Wahab, the family physician, stepped out with a somber expression on his face. It instantly changed to one of surprise and joy when he saw him standing there. He immediately embraced him and told him that it was good to see him.

"It is good to see you also, Sammy," Moses replied truthfully. He was one of the few men who didn't treat him like a leper just because his father did. "How is he doing?" he asked somberly.

Samuel stepped back with tears in his eyes. "Not good, not good at all, Moses," he said quietly. Moses made sure that his face showed the proper amount of sadness, but in reality, he was ecstatic because he would be in charge sooner rather than later. "Maybe I should go in and talk to him while I still can," he suggested anxiously, and this time the expression on his face wasn't fabricated at all. He was terrified.

Samuel looked at Moses sadly because he knew exactly what he was feeling. "You father loves you. He's been hard on you because he wants the best for you to make peace with him while you can." He smiled and patted him on the shoulder before taking his leave.

Moses gathered himself before quietly opening the door. He poked his head in and saw that his father was resting. He was surprised to see his father's bedroom turned into a hospital room with every machine imaginable available for his cae. Having second thoughts about disturbing his father's sleep, he started to step back out when the voice that used to make him wet the bed stopped him in his tracks.

"Stop peeking at me like a girl and come in here, boy."

Moses grimaced and bit his tongue to keep himself from saying something he might regret. He plastered a fake smile onto his face and stopped into the room, determined to not let his father get under his skin. "How are you, Father?" he asked politely. Ahmed tried to laugh at his son, but it turned into a cough that made one hurt just hearing it Moses stepped forward to help, but stopped in his tracks when his father lifted his hand, bidding him to stay where he was with a glare. After finally getting his cough under control, Ahmed pressed the button to lift himself into an upright position. He glazed at his son, looking him up and down as if cataloging everything he felt was wrong with his progeny.

Moses knew what he was doing because he had been doing it his whole life and he thought he was over letting his father control him, but as he wilted under his scathing look like he was some pimply teenager caught masturbating, he knew nothing could be further from the truth.

Ahmad smirked as he watched his heir, his only child, melt under his gaze. From the outside looking in, people would think he got a kick out of tormenting his son, but in reality, he was disgusted that he helped make a child so weak. He made it his mission to raise his son until he grew a backbone and showed that he was a true Bandele. "Where is my grandson?"

Moses thought about lying, but couldn't be sure if his father didn't already know the truth, so that's what he gave him. "He's in America with his mother and sister," he answered cruelly.

Ahmed raised an eyebrow at that and smirked at his son. "Why?" he asked sardonically. "Did she finally wake up and leave you?" He always wondered how his son got a woman of her caliber. "They just wanted to spend some more time in America while I came and checked on you," Moses said angrily.

Ahmed snorted derisively, not even bothering to hide his disdain. "Or maybe she finally saw through your facade and decided to leave you," he said disgustedly.

Moses wanted to refute his claims, but he couldn't, and that shamed him. All he could do was put his head down.

Ahmad looked at his son and shook his head in pity. He felt like he was being punished for all the terrible deeds he had committed in his life. "Oh Allah, why did you see fit to give me a cameloot for a son?" he asked in despair.

Moses abruptly looked up at his father and narrowed his eyes in an anger. "What did you just call me?" he asked seriously.

Ahmad chuckled when he saw the fire in his son. "I called you a camelot," he said in a voice that was clear of sickness. It seemed as if the anticipation of the long awaited confrontation with his wayward child had given him strength. "What, you thought I didn't know who you really were, boy?" He was indignant because his son had the nerve to act like he didn't know what he was talking about, "I really don't blame you, boy. I blame your mother, bless her heart. She was too soft with you, cuddled you too much, wouldn't let you get your hands dirty, and by the time she died, you were too far gone for me to do anything with. I tried everything, from hiring prostitutes to seeing shamans to fix you, but nothing could stop you from being a sissy boy." To his surprise, he had tears falling from his eyes.

Moses stared at his father blankly for a few seconds, seemingly uncomprehending anything that was just said, then with a roar he stepped over to his father's bed, grabbed a pillow from behind his head, and slammed it over his face, suffocating him. His father attempted to struggle, but in his feeble state, he was no match for his strength. After holding the pillow in place for a few extra seconds to make sure the deed was done, he pulled it away and looked at his father's face. Ironically, it looked as if he died with a smile on his face, and for one second he thought that his father might've actually been proud of him for once.

When the severity of what he had done kicked in, he almost panicked, but he forced himself to calm down and put everything back exactly like he found it. When he was sure nothing pointed to him, he alerted Samuel to his father's passing. The story he told was that they had made peace and his father took his last breath, holding his hand, knowing that the family was in good hands. He knew that the truth could never get out because if anyone ever found out that he had killed one of the most revered men in Nigeria, he would be fed to the hyenas.

# CHAPTER 22

Oura, Maine was a small, idyllic town that bordered the country of Canada. It was a place where the summer breeze felt like a lover's caress and a sip of lemonade felt like a pleasant kiss. Even though the winters were brutal, there was no lack of help, whether it was shoveling snow out of driveways, salting sidewalks or making sure everyone was fed and warm. Everyone pitched in and they did it with a smile. The crime rate was so low, it was basically nonexistent. The sheriff spent the majority of his time flirting with the pretty waitresses in the local diner as they kept him supplied with coffee and pie. The neighbors genuinely liked and trusted each other. They didn't give a second thought to going to bed with their doors unlocked. They felt safe in their little slice of American pie. So you could imagine what he would think if they knew that some of the world's biggest criminals were congregating right under their proverbial noses.

Eric Smith owned sixty acres of farmland that pushed right against the border that separated the good ol' US of A from Canada. It was ideal for the meeting he had called because it was secluded and far away from prying eyes. From the outside looking in, one couldn't tell that millions of dollars went into the renovation and restoration of the property. The exterior kept its rustic and weather worn look, but the interior was a different store. The security measures alone could rival the White House because in fact used the same firm that counseled with the Secret Service. He even had a private air strip built on the farthest reached of his property, which allowed him and or guests to fly in unnoticed without Customs' thorough inspections.

For some reason, he was looking forward to the setting of the minds because there seemed to be an impasse in regards to his advancement in the Council, and it was starting to make him resentful towards his puppets. He felt like it was time to utilize some new pieces. He felt like it was time to enter into the end game.

\*\*\*

The mood on the private jet was somber. Everyone knew how serious this summons was and wondered if they were walking into a trap. King held no illusions about what it was because he understood the power structure. Until you got your weight up, then you moved at the whims of others and as he looked into the faces of his brothers Czar, Majestic, and Pharaoh, he knew that they also understood this dynamic. He looked over at their parents and saw that their father was visibly agitated, but their mother was relaxed, almost serene, like she knew something no one else knew. They were all dressed to the nines in tuxedos with their mother rocking a Vera Wang ball gown because the messenger said that it was a black tie event. More than anything, the unknown bothered him because it was forcing him to move without a script, and for some, that would be a recipe for disaster. Luckily for him and his brothers, they could adapt to any situation. The pilot had just announced over the intercom that they would be landing in a few minutes, so it wouldn't be long before all was revealed and matters of life and death would be decided.

\*\*\*

Royalty was looking at her father with a puzzled look on her face. "Why are you so happy?" she asked suspiciously. The only time she had ever seen him smile was when someone was about to die.

Javier looked over at his daughter and let his smile fully bloom. He was on the verge of having everything he wanted and he couldn't help but smile when he thought about all of the master planning and manipulating he had to do just to get to his point. The only thing that could stop him was— well, nothing, because he was ten moves ahead of everyone else. "Tonight will be a major victory for the Salvatore family. And I hate you to thank for it," he added with a rare compliment.

Royalty was really looking at him crazy now. She had never heard anything close to a compliment come out of his mouth ever, and now here he was looking at her like she was the best thing to ever come out of his scrotum. She knew her father better than most, and there was no doubt in her mind that he was a sadistic, unremorseful megalomaniac who would stop at nothing to achieve his goals. For the first time in her life she belonged to a family, and she wouldn't let him destroy that. She looked at him again and rolled her eyes when she noticed him groping one of the stewardesses. She didn't even bother to respond to his insincere praise as she retired into her own head to plan her next moves, because if she calculated wrong, then she would be wiped off of the board.

***

As the jet taxied onto the runway, Shinah looked at her sons and felt her heart swell. A wave of sadness threatened to overwhelm her because she didn't have anything to do with the men they were, but that only strengthened her resolve to make sure she did right by them now. She wouldn't allow herself to fail them a second time.

"What's wrong, Ma?"

Shinah snapped out of her reverie every time she heard her son's voice with a smile. She looked up at Czar, who was gazing down at her with an expression of concern plastered onto his face. It still amazed her how far they had come in little over a year. When she popped back up in their lives, he had voiced the most anger, and she didn't begrudge him his feelings because she understood where he was coming from. So she wanted until he initiated contact and then had that conversation with him. After she was able to get him to see that she wasn't seeking forgiveness for leaving them because she knew that was wrong but that she wanted to get to know her sons and enjoy then while she still could, he forgave her and went out of his way to build their relationship. He was even the first to call her Ma, and it eased the paths of his brothers.

"Nothing's wrong, baby," she said sincerely. It wasn't, because in her mind, she had already made her move. Whether it worked or not was yet to be seen. "I just want you and your brothers to know that everything I've done and do from this point forward is for my children."

Czar was about to ask her what she meant when Sincere walked up, interrupting the moment. "I'm not feeling the whole mask and gloves bit," he said irritably, holding up a mask that looked like it might cover his whole face. It was white and made out of some hard plastic material that was actually kind of heavy. It reminded you of something one would wear to a masquerade ball.

"It's to protect everyone's identity from everyone else." Shinah patiently explained for what seemed like the hundredth time.

"Yeah, protect it from everybody except the person who summoned us, like sheep to a slaughter." He felt some type of way about being moved around like a pawn. It was a major blow to a man who always felt like he was the king of his own destiny. Shinah didn't bother to respond because they had been over this numerous times since the summons and she refused to address it again.

She stood up when their jet came to a complete stop and studied her family with a fierce expression upon her face. "Everyone on this plane leaves out of here the same way they walked in or none of us come out at all." She made sure to make eye contact with all of her boys to make certain they understood exactly what she meant. Once she was satisfied they did, she slid her mask over her face and exited the jet, where black on black Suburban SUVs were waiting to take them to their destination.

They all fell into step behind her, fully understanding the order she had given. In her world, they were all that mattered and if someone forgot, they had better remind them.

## CHAPTER 23

Chaka was ecstatic. Ever since she had told Majestic about her pregnancy, things had been good. She had been able to gradually remove herself from the life of a hit woman because for the first time in her life, she was dealing with a man she trusted with more than just her body, and it was rejuvenating to her spirit. Before Majestic, she had treated men as bodies to use or kill and nothing more, but now she loved the fact that he don't feel the need to crowd her or become overprotective since the baby news. It was like he sensed that she could take care of herself in his absence. He did not question her about her background, another thing she loved about him. They just fit and it was enough. Now she liked doing menial things like laundry, dishes, or cooking, but she didn't completely forego her past life. She still worked out religiously and trained in all of her different disciplines because it was too ingrained in her not to.

She had just finished a rigorous workout and was on her way to take a shower. She stopped in the master bedroom she shared with

Majestic to retrieve some items she had bought from Victoria's Secret earlier that day and immediately knew that someone had been there. Instinctively, she grabbed one of the numerous pistols she kept hidden around the house and proceeded to search every inch of it to make sure there were no surprises left for her. Satisfied that she was alone and that there were no explosives set up anywhere, she went back to the bedroom to retrieve the note she saw pinned to her headboard when she first realized that someone had violated their home. She grabbed a pair of latex gloves from the bathroom and put them on before gently removing the blade that was used to pin the note to the headboard. As she examined the blade, she felt her heart grow cold because she immediately recognized it as an assassin's knife. Typically hit men and women used them to send messages to potential victims to back off or stop what they were doing or the next visit wouldn't end so pleasantly.

She had even used them herself a few times, so she knew that she was dealing with a highly trained professional and was only alive because they wanted her to be. Almost as an afterthought, she picked the note up and read it.

Chaka, you don't know me and I don't know you, at least not yet, but you irrevocably changed my life when you murdered my husband. I don't fault you for his death. I've already expired the man responsible. In fact, I somewhat admire you for your kill because I know the skill level required to kill all men of my husband's caliber, but this does not change the fact that I must kill you for killing him. I am duty bound to do so. I granted you a reprieve until your child is born because as a rule, I don't harm children. Don't scoff at this gift I've given you. You have a chance to set your affairs in order and say your goodbyes, something I didn't get a chance to do with my husband. I could've killed

you on numerous occasions but I'm no coward. I want to look

you in your eyes before you die.

Jacta Alea Est

Chanel

Chaka smirked when she read how she ended the note. Jata Alex Est was Latin for 'The die is cast'. It's an expression people in her profession used to say whatever happens, happens. Death is an accepted risk for anyone in life, so you took whatever outcome to come your way as your just due. Either you were good enough or you weren't.

Reading the signature helped her put two and two together about who she had supposedly killed because after she expired someone, they became like smoke dissipating into the air. But she knew that Cha'nel was married to a fellow assassin and that they worked in tandem to complete jobs. His name was Rah'mel and he must've been the man she killed in the alleyway after she caught him following her on numerous occasions. She smiled as she remembered that showdown. Her smile withered a bit as she remembered underestimating him and it almost costing her dearly as it did the henchmen she had used to spring the trap. She wouldn't make the same mistake twice. This time she wouldn't play with her food.

***

Regina felt like she was living in alternate universes. In one, she was the happiest woman in the world. She had the man of her dreams and it was everything she could've ever hoped for. In the other, she was living a nightmare. She used to love going to work, but now she dreaded the thought of even stepping foot inside the place because Doctor Gunter had tuned into her tormentor. She thought that the sexual favor she had given him to get what she needed done would be a one-time thing, but she underestimated the devious nature of Stephan Gunter. Obviously he had memorized the information on the death certificate she had wanted him to sign and did some investigation into it after defiling her body. Even though he couldn't find out anything about the concrete he knew enough to get the proper people very, very interested in her activities, and that was something she couldn't afford to have happen.

So she was now being blackmailed into doing degrading sexual acts just keep Stephen from blowing the whistle and getting her fired or even worse, thrown in jail. She had tried cutting back on the hours to limit her contact with him, but he quickly caught on and nipped that in the bud. He basically demanded that she be available to him at least once a day, sometimes more, and it was starting to take a toll on her. But at least she was able to bring solace in Miguel. He turned out to be everything she ever imagined and more. He was nurturing, kind, protective, loving, and very handy. He was able to fix anything and made sure that their little apartment was running efficiently and smoothly. The first time they made love felt like heaven to her. He was gentle with her body, the complete opposite of what Stephen was with her. He took his time and made sure she was satisfied before reaching his own climax. Also, his body was to die for. She could almost have an orgasm just by looking at him. One of his favorite pastimes was working out and training. When she watched him go through his routines, she sensed a dangerousness to him, but instead of fear, she felt excitement knew that she was willing to go to the ends of the earth and do unspeakable things to keep him in her life.

That's why they were walking through the food bazaar trying to find him some fruit that only grew in Panama.

\*\*\*

Cha'nel was feeling nostalgic and missing her husband, so she was walking around the city of Miami, soaking up the culture. She had been there plenty of times, but it was always for a job. She had never been there for pleasure and since she had decided to give a Chaka a reprieve until after she gave birth, she wanted to relax – well, as much as one in her profession would at least. She was entering the food bazaar when movement out of the corner of her eye stopped her in her tracks.

\*\*\*

Regina was enjoying her time with Miguel, but she was ready to get back home to some earth shattering love. She was about to say that to Miguel when she got the sense that someone was staring at them. She looked around to see if she could spot any unwanted attention and saw a woman eyeing them intently. She looked up at Miguel to see if he noticed, but he was still looking at fruit. She looked back at the woman to find that she was still looking at him, but this time she was snarling. Regina didn't know who the woman was, but she instinctively knew that she was trouble. The only thing on her mind was getting home before something bad happened. She put a pained expression on her face and tugged on Miguel's arm to get his attention. When he saw the discomfort on her face, he immediately became concerned and attentive.

"What's wrong, mi amor?" he asked softly. "My stomach is hurting and I want to go home," she said with a fictitious moan. She surreptitiously looked over her shoulder to see that the woman hadn't made a move in their direction, but was still staring at them with that disconcerting frown on her face.

"All right, love. Let's get you to the car." Miguel started steering her through the crowd towards their car.

Regina sighed with relief when he didn't ask her too many questions before leading her to their car. She chanced another quick glance over her shoulder to make sure they weren't being followed.

Before the crowd closed around them, cutting off her view of the woman, she saw her still rooted in the same spot looking in their direction. She didn't know the woman, had never seen her before in her life, but she had a bad feeling that she would be seeing her again and she would do more than just stare.

***

Cha'nel felt like she was having a heart attack. She was having a hard time breathing and her chest felt tight. Her eyes had to be deceiving her because what she just saw couldn't have been real, but in her soul she knew it was. She knew her husband like she knew herself. She knew the way he breathed, the way he blinked, the way he talked, the way he moved, all of his mannerisms, and the man she had just seen on the arm of the Latina woman was undoubtedly her husband. Her mind was whirring with possibilities of why he was with her and not dead. The only conclusion her mind kept coming to was that she had been betrayed and made a fool. If that was the case, then he would rue the day he ever thought he could leave her for another women. She took until death do them part literally, and if he wanted to be a coward and fake his death to be with another woman, then she should grant his wish. But it would have to be in the next life because she planned on putting them both in the dirt.

## CHAPTER 24

When they exited their jet, Shinah, Sincere, and the boys were driven to what appeared to be a barn. After going through multiple rigorous security checks, they were led past house stables and farm equipment to a door that turned out to be a freight elevator. They all got on and waited quietly while they descended to what seemed to be the depths of the earth. They all looked at each other and wondered what exactly they were walking into when the elevator finally stopped its descent and the door was lifted. Everyone was surprised. What started out as a dusty old barn had been transformed into an elegant ballroom. There was a sense that you were in a different time with the chandeliers and French renaissance paintings. Everyone was wearing tuxedos or ball gowns with their mask firmly in place, keeping their identity a mystery to the other guests. They all accepted champagne from the serving tray offered by the waiter who met them at the door. Not knowing what else to do, they blended into the crowd and waited to see what happened next.

\*\*\*

By the time they were through the security checkpoints and in the elevator, Javier was visibly frustrated with what he deemed a lack of respect for his stature. He felt like he was being treated like a low level thug instead of the king he was and it was pissing him off. As soon as the elevator door was pulled up, he made a beeline for the champagne he saw waiting for him. He needed to take the edge off before their meeting.

Royalty watched her father's behavior around the room full of beautifully dressed and masked guests and wondered how many of those powerful wore the same expression as she did while watching her father knock back flute after flute of champagne like it was water. He held no illusions about how important this meeting was for her. She realized that her plan could potentially backfire and result in her death, but it was a risk she was willing to take to gain control of her design. It was past time she realized her own power. She was a Queen and she was done protecting the king.

***

"It seems as if all of the participants are here," Eric said to one of his most trusted subordinates. "Let's get this party started."

"Are you sure about this, Mr. Smith?" the subordinate asked nervously. His boss was known to have an explosive temper when his orders were questioned, but surprisingly, Eric smiled benignly. "In the business, your word is worth more than gold and I will never break mine. A marker was given and the person holding this marker has decided to cash it in. I told them I would give them anything in my power to give when and if they decided to call it in. Actually, what they asked me to do for them is a blessing for us both." He smirked as he thought about the ingenuity of the plan that had been presented to him. He was almost jealous that he didn't think of it himself. "So you see, I've never been more sure about anything in my life. Most times when advancement occurs, assets are lost, but in the very unique instance, both pieces attain their goals without any harm to themselves because they rely on each other for protection and help in times of need. Now make sure everyone is brought to the chamber." His tone brooked no further argument from his subordinate and his orders were immediately followed.

Eric waited until he was alone before he allowed himself to think about the enormity of what he was about to do. In the long, rich history of the Council, there had never been a woman with knowledge of the inner workings of the organization, let alone be able to call herself a member he treated as an equal. He would either be hailed as a visionary and allowed to enter into the inner circle, or he would be buried alive with enough oxygen to think about this foolish mistake. It was a risk he was willing to accept. He just hoped that she was ready because gaining a seat was one thing. Keeping it was something else entirely.

\*\*\*

Royalty was watching her father to make sure he didn't put them in a compromising position with his drinking when she felt someone step into her space. She turned to find a masked servant beckoning her to follow. She looked over her shoulder and saw that her father was also being led away from the rest of the guests. As she followed behind the servant, she wondered where her sister and nephews were because her plan wouldn't work without them. Regardless, she was going to make her move because her inaction was now verbal consent to be less than, and she wasn't going for the leash around her neck any longer.

\*\*\*

Shinah was watching her sons and wondered for the hundredth time if she was doing the right thing. She never imagined this life for them, but unseen forces played a part in their lives. She thought about everything she had been through over the last quarter century - the plotting, the sacrifices, the humiliations, and the unquenchable thirst for revenge - and wondered if it was worth it. Then she thought about the position her mother left them in and knew that she didn't have any choice in the matter. The scary thing was putting her faith in other people. For so long she had depended on herself to get by, but now she had to hope that the people she put her trust in were as capable as she was led to believe. When she looked around the room at her boys and the man she loved, she knew that whatever came her way, she would gladly face it with them.

***

Royalty breathed a sigh of relief when they finally arrived at their destination because it seemed as if they had ben walking forever. When she was led into the conference room, she suddenly felt an indescribable feeling in her heart when she saw her sister and nephews waiting for her. Everyone in the room wore masks the same as she did, but instinctively she knew that it was her family. She almost slipped up and called out Shinah's name, but her father stumbling into the room stopped her. She cast an angry glare at him over her shoulder before taking the seat nearest to her. She saw the servant who led them to the room leave and started to address the room, but before she could, a digitized voice came over the loud system that had to be hooked up to the room.

"The people in this room have made the last year of my life very interesting." The voice had everyone's attention. "None of you know me, but I know each and every one of you intimately. I'm a very busy individual who doesn't like wasting time. Anyone in this room who has wasted my time will not leave." The implication was clear. You either lived or died by his whim. "Javier Salvatore explained to me your reasons for wanting Mexico annexed and brought into my fold."

Javier wasn't used to being talked down to by anyone, but he understood that he needed to play his role to perfection to gain what he coveted so desperately. Then and only then would he assert his dominance and take his respect. "I think that it should be obvious why Mexico belongs under the North American banner instead of Latin America." As much as he tried, he couldn't keep the condescension out of his voice. He always felt like he was the smartest person in the room and he didn't see any reason to stop that train of thought now. "We border the US and we have raided this country that's being beneficial to both sides. I've been shipping tons of drugs across our borders for years, but if I'm allowed to expand my footprint, then the profit margin could be that much greater," he finished with a smile. No one could see it, but his arrogance shone like a lighthouse on a stormy night. "And the territory you've already accumulated in parts of Texas, Arizona, and California, who gave you permission to establish these strong holds in my kingdom?"

Javier was incredulous that this information was known. Those territories were to be his launching pads into the North American market, but now that seemed to be in jeopardy, with the revealing of this supposedly secret information, and if he didn't find a way to regain traction in this meeting, it might turn out bad for him. "Whoever informed you was surely mistaken," he said, lying through his teeth. "My forays into your kingdom are purely exploratory in nature, I assure you," he added with false bravado.

The disembodied voice didn't bother to respond as a projection screen descended from the ceiling. The lights were dimmed and a projector started flashing pictures upon the screen.

Javier knew that he was in trouble as soon as the first picture popped up onto the screen. His heart sank as picture after picture of his most trusted men in varying states of dismemberment flashed onto the screen. There was no denying the obvious now, not with the evidence right in front of his eyes. There was a rat in his organization. "I assure you that I have no knowledge of this," he protested feebly. "So now we add liar to your extensive list of violations," the voice said seriously. "Royalty, do you stand on your word by the penalty of death that the charges brought against your father are true?" The moment she had been waiting for all of her life was at hand. The realization dawning in her father's eyes that not only had he been beaten, but beaten by a species he despised, had no respect for, used, abused and threw away like trash, a woman, his daughter whom he overlooked constantly as she showed him repeatedly that she was better than then the men he continued to choose over here. The knowledge that his demise came from his own loins was too much to bear.

"Yes, they are true," she answered as a feeling washed over her that was almost indescribable, but felt orgasmic in nature.

"You bitch!" Javier screamed in rage as he jumped off his seat to attack his daughter.

Before he could reach her, individuals dressed in red robes and matching masks appeared as if out of nowhere and stopped him in his tracks.

"You're a dead puta!" he spat out her as he tried to break free from the clutches of the mashed individuals, but their grips held firm to him. "Your mother should've swallowed you," he snarled after realizing that he wasn't going anywhere.

"Enough!" the voice yelled. "Everyone here is under my protection, and my transgression against any of my guesses. Even so much as another insult will result in my people ending your life. Now please regain your composure, Mr. Salvatore, and retake your seat. The demand was unmistakable and required no response.

Javier was beyond furious. His anger had him shaking, but there wasn't anything to be gained from acting irrationally. He needed his wits about him now because he refused to believe that a mere woman could destroy him. Before reclaiming his seat, he cleared his throat and prepared to speak, but was stopped before he could even get started.

"Mr. Salvatore, if you're not clearing your throat to admit to your wrongs, then I suggest you not speak at all," the voice recommended.

Javier took a second to gather himself, but never took heed to what was said. "This woman…" He refused to claim her as his child any longer. "This women is in league with some other entity to destroy my organization. I do not believe that a mere woman could be capable of putting such an elaborate scheme together by herself. Give me leave to take her to a secluded area and I assure you that I will have the name of the real culprit behind this fiasco within the hour."

Royalty couldn't help herself. She chuckled at the absurdity of his claims.

Javier didn't react other than to cast a baleful glare at her.

"Mr. Salvatore, your closed mind has been your biggest weakness. Your daughter Royalty could've been your biggest asset if used correctly, but you repeatedly handicapped her by trusting less talented and less capable people than her. You thought she was lesser than because she was a woman and that was a colossal mistake. The Council has handcuffed itself with its antiquated way of thinking, but luckily for me, there are some who feel the way I feel and wouldn't mind being more inclusive. So with that being said, Royalty Salvatore you are now the king - or should I say Queen - of Mexico."

"What!" Javier shouted angrily as he jumped out of his seat in protest. "You have no authority to make such a move. Mexico belongs to group six, not group one," he said smugly, not bothering to mention that he just requested that Mexico be annexed into group one.

"Normally you would be right, but being that you violated Council bylaws and the violations were against my kingdom, I'm allowed to replace youth with anyone I deem fit to uphold the Council's reputation. Royalty Salvatore is who I'm choosing." "The Council will never vote a woman in," Javier stated firmly. "I want to appeal my expulsion," he added, claiming his Council right.

"Once again, normally you would receive your right to appeal, but sadly these are not normal circumstances and you don't have a lot of support on the Council," the voice said sternly. "You violated me, and I will not allow that to and maybe in the next life, you will learn to respect your betters."

Before Javier could comprehend exactly what was happening, he was grabbed by two of the red robed attendants. "No, no. You can't do this to me!" he screamed as he was led away. "You will fail, puta. I guarantee your mother should've swallowed!" he yelled at Royalty before being dragged out of the room and the door shutting behind him.

"Time is of the essence now so I won't waste any of it. The people in this room, Sincere, Loyalty, Royalty Salvatore, King Dominez, Majestic Livingston, Pharaoh Carter, Czar St. Pierre, and Shinah Lloyd, the trajectory of your lives has forever changed and you have to be ready for what's coming. The game is chess literally and the only outcomes are life and death. There will be no sympathy for this family and you can't give any. See the unseen and hear every whisper, because the only thing that will be a mark of your success or failure will be your preparation. Know your enemies as well as you know yourselves. Royalty, you have Mexico. It's up to you to keep it. The vote will happen in one year from today and if you're still alive on that date, then you will get the votes you need for admittance to the Council."

"Why are you helping us?" Royalty asked seriously. From everything she knew about the Council, this wasn't normal, especially with her being a female. "I think you will find your answer in what I'm about to say," the voice said. "I've done a lot in my time as king but as with any Shinah Lloyd as the new queen of the North American market." Royalty was stunned.

"With this move, you inherit a different set of problems. Your infrastructure will be your family. Understand that in this world, betrayal is as common as the sunrise. So you have to be vigilant. I've done unprecedented things here tonight, things that will upset a lot of traditionalists, but the support is there also. The only thing is that he will only acknowledge that support in public if you prove yourselves worthy. Your sons are a lead making quite a name for themselves. I've heard them called the four horsemen. They're your greatest weapons. Use their uniqueness to your advantage. With that being said, position your board and prepare for war. The first move has been made." The finality in the voice let them know that the conversation was at an end. "Who are you?" Royalty asked incredulously. She was in awe of what just happened.

Shinah stood up and snatched off her mask. "Save the question because as of right now, forces are being mobilized against us and our enemies are faceless. So we have to be vigilant and steadfast. We have to position ourselves to eliminate any and every threat because until we solidify our family, we're all in danger. We have Mexico, Jamaica, and the territories we already have a hold on. Prepare for it as if we have nothing to lose." She made eye contact with everyone in the room. "Because in reality, we don't."

\*\*\*

"The sharks will smell fresh blood in the water and look to feed." The subordinate stated the obvious. "What is the Council hoping to change?" he asked curiously.

"Not everything that is faced can be changed, but nothing can be changed until it is faced," Eric replied, quoting James Baldwin. "As confusing as it may seem to us, the Council does nothing without reason. Fire tempers steel or reveals its weaknesses." He indicated that he wanted to be left alone and the subordinate, knowing his boss, left the room.

Finally able to get lost in his thoughts uninterrupted, Eric wondered exactly what the inner circle of the Council was up to. When Shinah called in her marker, he immediately informed the Council and surprisingly, he was given the key to fulfill the marker. Despite his reservations, he went about his task as he did everything in his life: thoroughly. He genuinely likes Shinah, so he hoped that she and her family survived whatever the inner circle had planned for them. Their skies were about to rain blood. He just hoped they aren't afraid to get wet.

***

"Javier is dead."

"Good. He deserved much worse."

"Whats next?"

"A war, I presume."

"I mean for us."

"We're merely spectators at this point."

That answer was pondered before a response was given. "The Council will never accept two women into their ranks."

"The Council is dying and I, for one, refuse to die with it. Either we adapt and grow or we remain stagnant and perish."

Silence reigned for a few long minutes before another word was spoken. "To the victor goes the spoils."

"To the smartest goes the war."


To Be Continued...
King Killa 3
Coming Soon

**Lock Down Publications and Ca$h Presents** assisted
publishing packages.

BASIC PACKAGE $499
Editing
Cover Design
Formatting

UPGRADED PACKAGE $800
Typing
Editing
Cover Design Formatting

ADVANCE PACKAGE $1,200
Typing
Editing
Cover Design
Formatting
Copyright registration
Proofreading
Upload book to Amazon

LDP SUPREME PACKAGE $1,500
Typing
Editing
Cover Design
Formatting
Copyright registration
Proofreading
Set up Amazon account
Upload book to Amazon

Advertise on LDP Amazon and Facebook page ***Other services available upon request. Additional charges may apply
**Lock Down Publications P.O. Box 944 Stockbridge, GA 30281-9998 Phone # 470 303-9761**

# Submission Guideline

Submit the first three chapters of your completed manuscript to ldpsubmissions@gmail.com, subject line: Your book's title. The manuscript must be in a .doc file and sent as an attachment. Document should be in Times New Roman, double spaced and in size 12 font. Also, provide your synopsis and full contact information. If sending multiple submissions, they must each be in a separate email.

Have a story but no way to send it electronically? You can still submit to LDP/Ca$h Presents. Send in the first three chapters, written or typed, of your completed manuscript to:

**LDP: Submissions Dept**
**Po Box 944**
**Stockbridge, Ga 30281**

*DO NOT send original manuscript. Must be a duplicate.*

Provide your synopsis and a cover letter containing your full contact information.

Thanks for considering LDP and Ca$h Presents.

## <u>NEW RELEASES</u>

SUPER GREMLINS 2 by KING RIO

LOYALTY IS EVERYTHING 3 by MOLOTTI

HERE TODAY, GONE TOMORROW 2 by FLY ROCK

KING KILLA 2 by VINCENT "VITTO" HOLLOWAY

**Coming Soon from Lock Down Publications/Ca$h Presents**
BLOOD OF A BOSS **VI**
SHADOWS OF THE GAME II
TRAP BASTARD II
By **Askari**
LOYAL TO THE GAME **IV**
By **T.J. & Jelissa**
TRUE SAVAGE **VIII**
MIDNIGHT CARTEL IV
DOPE BOY MAGIC IV
CITY OF KINGZ III
NIGHTMARE ON SILENT AVE II
THE PLUG OF LIL MEXICO III
CLASSIC CITY II
By **Chris Green**
BLAST FOR ME **III**
A SAVAGE DOPEBOY III
CUTTHROAT MAFIA III
DUFFLE BAG CARTEL VII
HEARTLESS GOON VI By
**Ghost**
A HUSTLER'S DECEIT III KILL
ZONE II
BAE BELONGS TO ME III
TIL DEATH II
By **Aryanna**
KING OF THE TRAP III
By **T.J. Edwards**
GORILLAZ IN THE BAY V

3X KRAZY III

STRAIGHT BEAST MODE III

**De'Kari**

KINGPIN KILLAZ IV

STREET KINGS III

PAID IN BLOOD III

CARTEL KILLAZ IV

DOPE GODS III

**Hood Rich**

SINS OF A HUSTLA II

**ASAD**

YAYO V

Bred In The Game 2

**S. Allen**

THE STREETS WILL TALK II

**By Yolanda Moore**

SON OF A DOPE FIEND III

HEAVEN GOT A GHETTO III

SKI MASK MONEY III **By**

**Renta**

LOYALTY AIN'T PROMISED III **By**

**Keith Williams**

I'M NOTHING WITHOUT HIS LOVE II

SINS OF A THUG II

TO THE THUG I LOVED BEFORE II

IN A HUSTLER I TRUST II

**By Monet Dragun**

QUIET MONEY IV

EXTENDED CLIP III

THUG LIFE IV

By **Trai'Quan**

THE STREETS MADE ME IV

By **Larry D. Wright**

IF YOU CROSS ME ONCE III

ANGEL V

By **Anthony Fields**

THE STREETS WILL NEVER CLOSE IV

**By K'ajji**

HARD AND RUTHLESS III

KILLA KOUNTY IV **By**

**Khufu**

MONEY GAME III

**By Smoove Dolla**

JACK BOYS VS DOPE BOYS IV

A GANGSTA'S QUR'AN V

COKE GIRLZ II

COKE BOYS II

LIFE OF A SAVAGE V

CHI'RAQ GANGSTAS V SOSA

GANG IV

BRONX SAVAGES II

BODYMORE KINGPINS II

BLOOD OF A GOON II

**By Romell Tukes**

MURDA WAS THE CASE III **Elijah**

**R. Freeman**

AN UNFORESEEN LOVE IV

BABY, I'M WINTERTIME COLD III

By **Meesha**

QUEEN OF THE ZOO III

By **Black Migo**

KING KILLA III

**By Vincent "Vitto" Holloway**

BETRAYAL OF A THUG III

**By Fre$h**

THE BIRTH OF A GANGSTER IV

**By Delmont Player** TREAL

LOVE II

**By Le'Monica Jackson**

FOR THE LOVE OF BLOOD IV

**By Jamel Mitchell**

RAN OFF ON DA PLUG II **By**

**Paper Boi Rari**

HOOD CONSIGLIERE III

**By Keese**

PRETTY GIRLS DO NASTY THINGS II

**By Nicole Goosby**

LOVE IN THE TRENCHES II

**By Corey Robinson**

FOREVER GANGSTA III

**By Adrian Dulan**

SUPER GREMLIN III

**By King Rio**

CRIME BOSS II

**Playa Ray**

HERE TODAY GONE TOMORROW III
**By Fly Rock**
REAL G'S MOVE IN SILENCE II **By**
**Von Diesel**
GRIMEY WAYS IV
**By Ray Vinci**
BLOOD AND GAMES II
**By King Dream**
THE BLACK DIAMOND CARTEL II **By**
**SayNoMore**

**Available Now**

RESTRAINING ORDER **I & II**
By **CA$H & Coffee**
LOVE KNOWS NO BOUNDARIES **I II & III**
By **Coffee**
RAISED AS A GOON I, II, III & IV
BRED BY THE SLUMS I, II, III BLAST
FOR ME I & II
ROTTEN TO THE CORE I II III
A BRONX TALE I, II, III
DUFFLE BAG CARTEL I II III IV V VI

HEARTLESS GOON I II III IV V

A SAVAGE DOPEBOY I II DRUG

LORDS I II III

CUTTHROAT MAFIA I II

KING OF THE TRENCHES

By **Ghost**

LAY IT DOWN **I & II**

LAST OF A DYING BREED I II

BLOOD STAINS OF A SHOTTA I & II III

By **Jamaica**

LOYAL TO THE GAME I II III

LIFE OF SIN I, II III

By **TJ & Jelissa**

BLOODY COMMAS I & II

SKI MASK CARTEL I  II & III

KING OF NEW YORK I II,III IV V

RISE TO POWER I II III

COKE KINGS I II III IV V

BORN HEARTLESS I II III IV

KING OF THE TRAP I II By

**T.J. Edwards**

IF LOVING HIM IS WRONG…I & II

LOVE ME EVEN WHEN IT HURTS I II III

By **Jelissa**

WHEN THE STREETS CLAP BACK I & II III

THE HEART OF A SAVAGE I II III IV

MONEY MAFIA I II

LOYAL TO THE SOIL I II III

By **Jibril Williams**

A DISTINGUISHED THUG STOLE MY HEART I II & III

LOVE SHOULDN'T HURT I II III IV

RENEGADE BOYS I II III IV

PAID IN KARMA I II III

SAVAGE STORMS I II III

AN UNFORESEEN LOVE I II III

BABY, I'M WINTERTIME COLD I II

By **Meesha**

A GANGSTER'S CODE I &, II III

A GANGSTER'S SYN I II III THE

SAVAGE LIFE I II III

CHAINED TO THE STREETS I II III

BLOOD ON THE MONEY I II III

A GANGSTA'S PAIN I II III

**By J-Blunt**

PUSH IT TO THE LIMIT

By **Bre' Hayes**

BLOOD OF A BOSS **I, II, III, IV, V**

SHADOWS OF THE GAME

TRAP BASTARD

By **Askari**

THE STREETS BLEED MURDER **I, II & III**

THE HEART OF A GANGSTA I II& III By

**Jerry Jackson**

CUM FOR ME I II III IV V VI VII VIII

An **LDP Erotica Collaboration**

BRIDE OF A HUSTLA **I  II & II**

THE FETTI GIRLS **I, II& III**

CORRUPTED BY A GANGSTA I, II III, IV

BLINDED BY HIS LOVE

THE PRICE YOU PAY FOR LOVE I, II ,III

DOPE GIRL MAGIC I II III

By **Destiny Skai**

WHEN A GOOD GIRL GOES BAD

By **Adrienne**

THE COST OF LOYALTY I II III **By**

**Kweli**

A GANGSTER'S REVENGE **I II III & IV**

THE BOSS MAN'S DAUGHTERS I II III IV V

A SAVAGE LOVE **I & II**

BAE BELONGS TO ME I II

A HUSTLER'S DECEIT I, II, III

WHAT BAD BITCHES DO I, II, III

SOUL OF A MONSTER I II III KILL ZONE

A DOPE BOY'S QUEEN I II III

TIL DEATH

By **Aryanna**

A KINGPIN'S AMBITON

A KINGPIN'S AMBITION **II**

I MURDER FOR THE DOUGH

By **Ambitious**

TRUE SAVAGE I II III IV V VI VII

DOPE BOY MAGIC I, II, III

MIDNIGHT CARTEL I II III

CITY OF KINGZ I II

NIGHTMARE ON SILENT AVE

THE PLUG OF LIL MEXICO I II

CLASSIC CITY

By **Chris Green**

A DOPEBOY'S PRAYER

By **Eddie "Wolf" Lee**

THE KING CARTEL **I, II & III**

By **Frank Gresham**

THESE NIGGAS AIN'T LOYAL **I, II & III**

By **Nikki Tee**

GANGSTA SHYT **I II &III**

By **CATO**

THE ULTIMATE BETRAYAL   By

**Phoenix**

BOSS'N UP **I , II & III**

By **Royal Nicole**

I LOVE YOU TO DEATH

By **Destiny J**

I RIDE FOR MY HITTA

I STILL RIDE FOR MY HITTA By

**Misty Holt**

LOVE & CHASIN' PAPER

By **Qay Crockett**

TO DIE IN VAIN

SINS OF A HUSTLA

By **ASAD**

BROOKLYN HUSTLAZ

By **Boogsy Morina**

BROOKLYN ON LOCK I & II

By **Sonovia**

GANGSTA CITY

By **Teddy Duke**

A DRUG KING AND HIS DIAMOND I & II III

A DOPEMAN'S RICHES

HER MAN, MINE'S TOO I, II

CASH MONEY HO'S

THE WIFEY I USED TO BE I II

PRETTY GIRLS DO NASTY THINGS

**By Nicole Goosby**

TRAPHOUSE KING **I II & III**

KINGPIN KILLAZ I II III

STREET KINGS I II

PAID IN BLOOD **I II**

CARTEL KILLAZ I II III

DOPE GODS I II

By **Hood Rich**

LIPSTICK KILLAH **I, II, III**

CRIME OF PASSION I II & III

FRIEND OR FOE I II III By

**Mimi**

STEADY MOBBN' **I, II, III**

THE STREETS STAINED MY SOUL I II III

By **Marcellus Allen**

WHO SHOT YA **I, II, III**

SON OF A DOPE FIEND I II

HEAVEN GOT A GHETTO I II

SKI MASK MONEY I II
**Renta**
GORILLAZ IN THE BAY **I II III IV**
TEARS OF A GANGSTA I II
3X KRAZY I II
STRAIGHT BEAST MODE I II
**DE'KARI**
TRIGGADALE I II III
MURDAROBER WAS THE CASE I II
**Elijah R. Freeman**
GOD BLESS THE TRAPPERS I, II, III
THESE SCANDALOUS STREETS I, II, III
FEAR MY GANGSTA I, II, III IV, V
THESE STREETS DON'T LOVE NOBODY I, II
BURY ME A G I, II, III, IV, V
A GANGSTA'S EMPIRE I, II, III, IV
THE DOPEMAN'S BODYGAURD I II
THE REALEST KILLAZ I II III
THE LAST OF THE OGS I II III **Tranay**
**Adams**
THE STREETS ARE CALLING
**Duquie Wilson**
MARRIED TO A BOSS I II III
**By Destiny Skai & Chris Green**
KINGZ OF THE GAME I II III IV V VI VII
CRIME BOSS
**Playa Ray**
SLAUGHTER GANG I II III
RUTHLESS HEART I II III

**By Willie Slaughter** FUK
SHYT
**By Blakk Diamond**
DON'T F#CK WITH MY HEART I II **By**
**Linnea**
ADDICTED TO THE DRAMA I II III
IN THE ARM OF HIS BOSS II
**By Jamila**
YAYO I II III IV
A SHOOTER'S AMBITION I II
BRED IN THE GAME
**By S. Allen**
TRAP GOD I II III
RICH $AVAGE I II III
MONEY IN THE GRAVE I II III
**By Martell Troublesome Bolden**
FOREVER GANGSTA I II
GLOCKS ON SATIN SHEETS I II
**By Adrian Dulan**
TOE TAGZ I II III IV
LEVELS TO THIS SHYT I II
IT'S JUST ME AND YOU I II
**By Ah'Million**
KINGPIN DREAMS I II III
RAN OFF ON DA PLUG
**By Paper Boi Rari**
CONFESSIONS OF A GANGSTA I II III IV

CONFESSIONS OF A JACKBOY I II III **By**
**Nicholas Lock**
I'M NOTHING WITHOUT HIS LOVE
SINS OF A THUG
TO THE THUG I LOVED BEFORE
A GANGSTA SAVED XMAS
IN A HUSTLER I TRUST
**By Monet Dragun**
CAUGHT UP IN THE LIFE I II III
THE STREETS NEVER LET GO I II III
**By Robert Baptiste**
NEW TO THE GAME I II III
MONEY, MURDER & MEMORIES I II III
By **Malik D. Rice**
LIFE OF A SAVAGE I II III IV
A GANGSTA'S QUR'AN I II III IV
MURDA SEASON I II III
GANGLAND CARTEL I II III
CHI'RAQ GANGSTAS I II III IV
KILLERS ON ELM STREET I II III
JACK BOYZ N DA BRONX I II III
A DOPEBOY'S DREAM I II III
JACK BOYS VS DOPE BOYS I II III
COKE GIRLZ
COKE BOYS
SOSA GANG I II III
BRONX SAVAGES
BODYMORE KINGPINS

BLOOD OF A GOON **By**

**Romell Tukes**

LOYALTY AIN'T PROMISED I II **By**

**Keith Williams**

QUIET MONEY I II III

THUG LIFE I II III

EXTENDED CLIP I II

A GANGSTA'S PARADISE

By **Trai'Quan**

THE STREETS MADE ME I II III

By **Larry D. Wright**

THE ULTIMATE SACRIFICE I, II, III, IV, V, VI

KHADIFI

IF YOU CROSS ME ONCE I II

ANGEL I II III IV

IN THE BLINK OF AN EYE By

**Anthony Fields**

THE LIFE OF A HOOD STAR

By **Ca$h & Rashia Wilson**

THE STREETS WILL NEVER CLOSE I II III

By **K'ajji**

CREAM I II III

THE STREETS WILL TALK

By **Yolanda Moore**

NIGHTMARES OF A HUSTLA I II III

BLOOD AND GAMES

By **King Dream**

CONCRETE KILLA I II III

VICIOUS LOYALTY I II III **By**

**Kingpen**

HARD AND RUTHLESS I II

MOB TOWN 251

THE BILLIONAIRE BENTLEYS I II III

REAL G'S MOVE IN SILENCE

**By Von Diesel**

GHOST MOB

**Stilloan Robinson**

MOB TIES I II III IV V VI

SOUL OF A HUSTLER, HEART OF A KILLER I II III

GORILLAZ IN THE TRENCHES I II III

THE BLACK DIAMOND CARTEL

**By SayNoMore**

BODYMORE MURDERLAND  I II III

THE BIRTH OF A GANGSTER I II III

**By Delmont Player**

FOR THE LOVE OF A BOSS

**By C. D. Blue**

MOBBED UP I II III IV

THE BRICK MAN I II III IV V

THE COCAINE PRINCESS I II III IV V VI VII VIII IX X

SUPER GREMLIN I II

**By King Rio**

KILLA KOUNTY I II III IV

**By Khufu**

MONEY GAME I II **By**

**Smoove Dolla**

A GANGSTA'S KARMA I II III
**By FLAME** KING OF THE
TRENCHES I II III by **GHOST &
TRANAY ADAMS**
QUEEN OF THE ZOO I II
By **Black Migo**
GRIMEY WAYS I II III
**By Ray Vinci**
XMAS WITH AN ATL SHOOTER
**By Ca$h & Destiny Skai**
KING KILLA I II
**By Vincent "Vitto" Holloway**
BETRAYAL OF A THUG I II
**By Fre$h**
THE MURDER QUEENS I II III
**By Michael Gallon** TREAL
LOVE
**By Le'Monica Jackson**
FOR THE LOVE OF BLOOD I II III
**By Jamel Mitchell**
HOOD CONSIGLIERE I II
**By Keese**
PROTÉGÉ OF A LEGEND I II III
LOVE IN THE TRENCHES
**By Corey Robinson**
**BORN IN THE GRAVE I II III**
**By Self Made Tay**
**MOAN IN MY MOUTH**
**SANCTIFIED AND HORNY**

**By XTASY**

**TORN BETWEEN A GANGSTER AND A GENTLEMAN**

By J-BLUNT & Miss Kim

LOYALTY IS EVERYTHING I II III

**Molotti**

HERE TODAY GONE TOMORROW I II

**By Fly Rock**

PILLOW PRINCESS

**By S. Hawkins**

NAÏVE TO THE STREETS

WOMEN LIE MEN LIE I II III

GIRLS FALL LIKE DOMINOS

STACK BEFORE YOU SPURLGE

FIFTY SHADES OF SNOW I II III

**By A. Roy Milligan**

SALUTE MY SAVAGERY I II  **By**

**Fumiya Payne**

<u>**BOOKS BY LDP'S CEO, CA$H**</u>

TRUST IN NO MAN

TRUST IN NO MAN 2

TRUST IN NO MAN 3

BONDED BY BLOOD

SHORTY GOT A THUG

THUGS CRY

THUGS CRY 2

THUGS CRY 3

TRUST NO BITCH

TRUST NO BITCH 2

TRUST NO BITCH 3

TIL MY CASKET DROPS

RESTRAINING ORDER

RESTRAINING ORDER 2

IN LOVE WITH A CONVICT

LIFE OF A HOOD STAR

XMAS WITH AN ATL SHOOTER